The healing hippo of hinode park

Also by Michiko Aoyama

What You Are Looking For Is in the Library

The healing hippo of hinode park

A Novel

Michiko Aoyama

Translated from the Japanese by Takami Nieda

HANOVER
SQUARE
PRESS

HANOVER
SQUARE
PRESS™

Recycling programs
for this product may
not exist in your area.

ISBN-13: 978-1-335-01633-1

The Healing Hippo of Hinode Park

Hanover Square Press
22 Adelaide St. West, 41st Floor
Toronto, Ontario M5H 4E3, Canada
HanoverSqPress.com

HarperCollins Publishers
Macken House, 39/40 Mayor Street Upper,
Dublin 1, D01 C9W8, Ireland
www.HarperCollins.com

Printed in U.S.A.

The
healing
hippo
of
hinode
park

1

Kanato's Head

I turned the 6 into an 8.

And the 1 into a 9.

In a matter of seconds, my world was transformed.
I clicked the cap back on the red felt-tip pen.

The 61 I scored on my English test was now an 89.

This rewritten reality seemed much more suited
to who I really was. It was all good, I told myself.

After all, there was no way I could be *this* stupid.

~

Last year, during the summer of my third year in junior high school, my father announced that he was buying a condominium.

'In a brand-new building. Isn't that great, Kanato?' His voice sounded higher than usual and filled with pride as he shared the news at dinner, beer foam glistening on his lip. It had always been a dream of my father's, who had lived for years in employee housing, to own a home of his own.

He told us the name of the nearest train station, about an hour from our current home and closer to Tokyo. My mother added that an electronics-manufacturing factory would be demolished for a new five-storey condominium building.

My parents decided on a first-floor unit with a yard—a rarity for a condo, which was a plus. Having a garden where my father could get his hands dirty was essential, and they'd been looking at older houses for this reason, when they first discovered this property. It was close to the train station and with a supermarket and plenty of restaurants nearby, checking off both my parents' budget and location requirements. They couldn't be happier.

Advance Hill. Construction of this ostentatiously

named condominium was scheduled for completion in March, so my parents set a date to move after my junior high school graduation.

Until then, I attended a public school in a quiet suburb. Not to sound immodest, but I was a top student.

Life in junior high was lax. Tepid. If I'm being honest, I don't recall ever studying. If I paid attention in class, I could flip through the textbook before a test and guess what would be on it. All I had to do was submit my worksheets on time, and I had a row of A's on my report card.

Watching students passing around notes or sleeping with their mouths open during class, I couldn't understand why they would be jealous that I was 'smart'. It was no wonder their grades were horrible.

With the move closer to Tokyo, I decided to apply to a preparatory high school in the city.

Other than me, no one else at my junior high had applied to that school. Seeing my mother's satisfied smile when my homeroom teacher mentioned I should be able to qualify for recommendation-based admission made me happy, too. I passed the entrance exam without much difficulty, freeing me from that particular worry before the year ended.

I quit the cram school I'd been attending since grade school and spent the year-end holidays reading manga and playing video games. Busy shopping for curtains and furniture, my parents made no comment on how much I was playing.

As graduation approached, the homeroom teacher said something about how I would miss my old friends, but I didn't particularly feel that way. I had classmates that I got on with, but I wouldn't say they were friends that I could open up to, and I never felt like I belonged.

Since I didn't have anyone to miss, what I felt, if anything, was free.

A new home, a new life. I entered high school with high hopes, fully expecting to find a friend who I could truly connect with.

As soon as the term began, however, I realized I didn't fit into any cliques.

The popular crowd was too intimidating, the guys who were always arguing a little too loudly were unapproachable, the nerds buried in their study-aid books were hard to talk to. In retrospect, my classmates from junior high school were much easier to talk to.

But more than anything, it was the midterm exams that delivered the biggest blow.

For starters, each test had too many problems, so I couldn't finish within the allotted time. Not only was it tricky to predict what would appear on the test, but some questions weren't even covered in class. The teacher said anything considered part of the general education requirements was fair game, or something like that. When the exam period was over, all my tests came back with low scores. My pride was in tatters. A few days later, we received a slip of paper listing students' rankings.

Thirty-fifth out of forty-two students.

Since I had never received a ranking lower than third, I was shocked.

Something's wrong, I thought. *I can't possibly be this stupid.*

There was no way I could show the results to my mother. I played innocent for as long as I could until she finally asked, 'How did you do on the midterms?' I showed her my exam sheets, making sure to leave out any mention of student rankings.

As she looked at the scores, the crease between her brows grew deeper. To keep myself from falling into that furrow, I hastily said, 'The average scores were low.'

The crease on her face relaxed slightly.

'The exams were incredibly hard. Everyone was struggling.'

That was a lie. The only exam that I'd managed to score above average on was in English, my best subject.

'Eh, sounds about right for your first exams in high school,' my father intervened. He then mentioned buying some fertilizer at the hardware store, and thankfully, my mother handed back the exam sheets and started talking to him.

It wasn't so much that he had sent me a lifeboat as that he didn't care. My father never took an interest in me, much less my grades, and despite his ever-present smile, he never praised me for anything. Still, I was grateful to him for changing the subject.

I told myself I'd do better on the final exams, but all my motivation had vanished.

I found myself in an awful predicament. The truth was that I'd sensed the difference in my skill level between my classmates and me during class. The gap was so wide that it felt impossible to catch up.

The pace of the lessons was fast, and I frequently couldn't answer when the teacher called on me. Growing impatient with my silence, the teacher called on another student, and when that student answered correctly, I wanted to crawl into a hole and die. It seemed simply paying attention in class, like I had in junior high school, wasn't cutting it anymore.

As I struggled to concentrate, my final exams came and went. Now, two days after finishing them, I had come out of the room completely overwhelmed. I felt like I had done even worse than before. Everyone else seemed like a genius. They all had breezy looks on their faces.

The few days' wait for the student rankings to come out was more nerve-racking than the wait for the high school acceptance.

Yesterday, we received the results of the English exam.

A 61. The average was 62. I had failed to exceed the average in my best subject.

More speechless than disappointed, I was numbed.

As soon as I got home, my mother asked when I was getting my tests back, and I panicked.

That was the moment I went back to my room and picked up the red pen.

And turned the 6 into an 8.

And the 1 into a 9.

'I got my English test back,' I said now, and showed her the score.

The 89 was displayed prominently on the answer sheet.

'The average was sixty-two.' My voice was confident because it wasn't a lie.

Narrowing her eyes, she replied, 'Good for you, Kanato! You must have tried very hard.'

'Uh, yeah,' I answered.

The inside of my mouth tingled like I'd swallowed some bitter medicine. Inwardly, I was screaming. *Why? How?*

How did I get so dumb?

~

The next day, when I arrived at my train stop after school, I couldn't bring myself to go straight home, so I decided to take a detour.

I turned off the main road on to a backstreet and

into a residential neighbourhood. Amid the rows of houses stood a well-worn building with a store occupying the first floor. The words 'Sunrise Cleaning' were outlined against the red overhang. There was a soda vending machine out front; fluorescent lights shone through the glass storefront.

I carried on walking until I reached a cluster of rundown beige-looking apartment complexes distinguishable only by the enormous numbers on the sides of the buildings. It was late evening, but there were still several futons hanging over balcony railings to dry.

I walked along the narrow promenade until I got to a small playground nestled among the apartments. At the entrance stood a stone slab with the words 'Hinode Park' engraved into it.

It was a small, gravelled playground, fitted out with the usual items you might expect to find in a park: a set of swings, a slide, a sandbox and a bench.

No one else was around except for me. As I stepped into the playground to rest on a bench, an animal-shaped figure in the corner caught my eye.

A hippopotamus.

It was one of those stationary animal rides you just

sat on. The orange paint, browning in places, was starting to peel off. The exposed concrete underneath created a mottled appearance, all quite normal for a hippo. Its oval-shaped eyes were turned slightly upward, the black of its pupils also peeling in spots, giving it a teary-eyed look like something out of a manga. A smile spread across its face and curled up at the corners. The upturned nostrils perched atop two mounds lent the hippo a ridiculously carefree expression.

I approached it to get a closer look. With a marker, someone had scribbled 'STUPID' on the back of its head. Calling a hippo *stupid* for being slow-moving— what a cheap shot! Seeing such a violent scrawl broke my heart.

And yet, the hippo was smiling. Maybe it couldn't see the graffiti because it was written on the back of its head. Maybe the hippo didn't know it was being slandered.

With a deep sigh, I tried to rub out the word with my fingers. The letters, likely written in permanent marker, weren't about to come out so easily.

I took out a pencil case from my knapsack and tried rubbing the marker out with an eraser. It was no use. My efforts produced only eraser crumbs as the word stubbornly remained emblazoned on the hippo.

This filled me with an urge to get rid of the graffiti by any means necessary. I couldn't help but see myself as the hippo, helpless to do anything about the 'stupid' label he was stuck with.

I came up with the idea of painting over it in a similar colour.

I should have some orange lacquer paint that I'd used to colour a plastic model when I was in junior high back home.

'I'll bring it tomorrow, okay?' I said out loud to the hippo.

The stumpy hippo looked up at me, teary-eyed and smiling.

~

The following day, as soon as school ended, I rushed straight for the park, a bottle of lacquer paint stuck in my knapsack.

I stepped inside the park to find a girl in a school uniform pumping her legs on a swing. Noting the blue ribbon waving in front of her white blouse, I realized she was from my school.

She was smiling and gazing into the distance, her cheeks flushed. Her face felt familiar.

That was it. She was a classmate—Shizukuda-san, I think it was. I'd never spoken to her before and couldn't remember her first name. But her naturally curly hair and her loud, husky voice had stuck in my mind.

As I turned back towards the gate, Shizukuda-san looked over and caught my eye. For some reason, she smiled at me as if we'd known each other for ages.

My heart skipped a beat. I dipped my head in greeting.

She brought the swing to a stop. 'You're Kanato Miyahara!'

My heart skipped again. She knew my full name!

'What are you doing here? Do you live in the neighbourhood?'

'Uh, yeah,' I said. 'The condominiums called Advance Hill.'

'I know that place! The new building on the hill. Oh, wow.'

She hopped off the swing and came up to me. I unthinkingly did the same.

'I've been living here since I was a kid. Building six.'

Her building faced the park. Struggling to keep the conversation going, I asked, 'Do you like the swings?'

She looked into the distance again and answered seriously, '*Like?* More like it helps me to decompress and recharge. When everything feels like a lot sometimes.'

Decompress and recharge?

As I struggled to respond, Shizukuda-san turned towards the corner of the playground.

'Kabahiko!' she said, as if she were calling to a pet dog or cat, and walked up to the hippo.

'Kabahiko?' I parroted back, and Shizukuda-san nodded.

'Yep. The name of this guy here.'

She turned to face me. 'Kabahiko is an amazing hippo. People say that if you touch the area of his body that you want to make better on yours, he'll provide a cure.'

13

I was stunned. Who knew that a miserable-looking hippo had the power to bestow such benefits?

Putting up a finger, she added, 'They call him Healing Kabahiko.'

'Healing Kabahiko?'

'Get it?' she said. 'Because Kaba-*hiko* sounds like *hippo*.'

I huffed, not because it was funny but because all the tension seemed to drain out of me.

Shizukuda-san then explained, 'It's this old rumour from round here. Something I grew up hearing about. The lady at Sunrise Cleaning said she patted Kabahiko's back, and it cured her herniated disk.'

Sunrise Cleaning. I remembered passing it on the way here.

I quickly scanned my surroundings. At dusk, there was no one else inside the shadowy playground. Perhaps noticing the suspicious look on my face, Shizukuda-san turned her head.

'Well, not that it's all over the news or anything. There's no scientific basis for it. I mean, it's just a boring hippo in this boring park.'

She was right. Both the subject and location

weren't buzzworthy enough for such a rumour to go viral. Besides, the park didn't have any other attractions that would make anyone want to come here.

Still, it was good to know.

I wanted to be cured of my stupidity. I wanted people to tell me that I was smart again.

Shizukuda-san crouched in front of Kabahiko. The hippo seemed to hold a special meaning for her, who'd lived here for years.

'Please make me beautiful,' she prayed, touching Kabahiko's face.

'Does it work on those kinds of things, too?' I asked, suppressing the burning question in my heart: *Isn't that more a wish than a healing?*

Seeming to read my mind, she stood up with her hands balled into fists. 'I was adorable when I was little, you know. When I was four, a scout stopped my mother and me on the street and asked if I wanted to go into modelling.'

'Okay . . .'

'It's true! Even though I look like this now . . .'

She cast her eyes down and pouted.

Like *this*? Now that I had a chance to talk to her, I thought she was cute.

15

I made sure to tuck that thought away in a corner of my heart where she couldn't read it. She gave Kabahiko's face a good rub.

'Please, Kabahiko! Heal my face!'

Trying to match her energy, I put a hand on Kabahiko's head.

'Please, Kabahiko! Heal my brain!'

'Your brain?'

Shizukuda-san chuckled, and the mood between us relaxed. I felt a sense of relief that I hadn't experienced in a while.

Like tangled threads unravelling, I began to speak my thoughts.

'I used to be a pretty good student when I was in junior high. So I was shocked that I bombed the midterm exams. When the final exams were just as hard, I lost all confidence. There was so much covered on the geography test.'

'I'm horrible at geography,' Shizukuda-san piped up. 'I'm more of a science person, if anything. When I found out at the entrance ceremony that our homeroom teacher would be Mr Yashiro, the geography teacher, I almost cried,' she said, making a face.

Finally, I found a classmate with whom I could have a frank conversation. Although, bonding over our lack of academic skills wasn't exactly the ideal scenario.

'But you're really good in English, Miyahara-kun! Your pronunciation is excellent.'

Well, yeah, but . . .

'But I didn't even rank in the top five on the midterms. I used to be first in junior high.'

The instant the words left my mouth, I wanted to run away in shame.

What a colossally cocky thing to say.

I was talking like I'd ranked sixth or seventh in the class. I was being pathetic, trying to impress Shizukuda-san by pretending to be a top student.

I braced myself, worried that she might be put off by what I'd said, but she started to cackle, 'I'm not even in the top ten!'

She climbed onto Kabahiko's back. Her legs sticking out from her skirt were so blindingly pale that I had to look away.

Shizukuda-san fiddled with her hair, muttering to herself, 'I think rankings are cruel. If you ask forty-two students to do the same thing at once, someone is going to come in forty-second. There's always going to be a forty-second. You can't just make that last spot disappear.'

When I found out I was thirty-fifth, I had thought that there were *only* seven students behind me. But after a fleeting moment, I had thought, there were *still* seven students behind me.

There was no telling what would happen next time. I might easily find myself sitting in the forty-second spot you couldn't make go away.

Shizukuda-san continued, 'Rankings are only important for people confined inside their tiny world.'

The way she said *only* stung my chest.

'An Olympic runner is already awesome just for being at the Olympics, but winning at the Games doesn't necessarily make you the best runner in the world—because somewhere in a secluded corner of the world so deep in the mountains you can't even get a signal, there could be a boy that runs faster than anyone.'

'What country is that?' I asked.

'I don't know. I'm just imagining. That boy loves to run, like really, and he couldn't care less about competing or about accolades or fame.'

I tried to imagine the boy she described. He was running through the fields and through mountains, half-naked and barefoot. I felt certain that a fast boy like that surely existed.

He ran and ran to his heart's content, blissfully unaware that he was the fastest human in the world, never seeking such a title in the first place.

And then, I was reminded of a certain character in a popular manga.

The comic, which had also been adapted into an anime, was called *Black Manhole*. It was a story about a monster living in the sewer system, which also featured a character named Terra, who was superfast. He ran at an incredible speed, without competing against anyone, completely absorbed in the act of running itself.

'He sounds like Terra,' I said. 'From *Bura-man*.'

'*Bura-man*? Oh, you mean *Black Manhole*. I know the anime on TV, but I haven't read the manga. Sounds good, though.' She glanced at her watch. 'Well, I have to head off to work.'

'You work part-time?'

'At a restaurant called Okonomiyaki Nikko. It's a lot of fun.'

Our high school didn't prohibit students from working part-time, although prior notification was required.

At least Shizukuda-san was enjoying high school life—hanging out and working part-time.

As she stood up, she caught a glimpse of Kabahiko's head and gasped. 'Ugh, someone wrote "stupid" on Kabahiko's head.'

I peered down at the letters along with her.

'I know. I tried rubbing it out, but it seems to have been written in permanent marker. I thought about painting over it. I brought some lacquer paint for colouring plastic models in a similar colour.'

I took out the bottle from my knapsack.

When I held it up next to the hippo, it was a much lighter shade than his colour. Painting over the graffiti in that colour might have the opposite effect of drawing attention to it. Besides—

'We could paint over it, but it's sad knowing the words will still be there underneath,' I said.

Hiding it wasn't the same as removing it. Painting over it wouldn't make it disappear like it was never there.

Shizukuda-san tilted her head sideways. 'I wonder if nail polish remover would do the trick. I could bring some next time.'

'But won't that take off the paint along with the ink? I'd hate to see him looking patchier than he already is.'

'Yeah, you're right. After so many hands have touched him, only to be neglected like this. It's just too sad.'

She patted Kabahiko gently, not to have her wishes fulfilled but out of genuine affection for the hippo.

She's a good person.

As soon as the thought came into my head, she looked up at me. 'You're a good person,' she said, as if she had read my mind. I felt my spirits lift, and the words 'I can lend you *Bura-man* if you like' tumbled out of my mouth.

'Really?' Her eyes lit up.

I owned every volume of *Bura-man* that had come out so far. Since there were more than twenty volumes in the series, I decided to give her a bunch at a time. I promised to bring her the first five tomorrow, Friday, so she could have them to read over the weekend.

'Really? That sounds great!'

Shizukuda-san smiled and jogged happily in place.

Watching her made me want to kick my feet in excitement, too.

Maybe Shizukuda-san would be my friend. My first friend since starting high school.

~

When I returned to the condominium, I bumped into a mother and her daughter at the entrance.

The girl might have been about five years old. I'd seen them several times before. They were residents of the apartment.

The mother greeted me with a smile. 'Hello.' She turned to the girl and prompted, 'What do you say, Mizuho?'

The girl named Mizuho gave me a dainty bow. 'Hi.'

'Hello.'

I bowed to them both.

The girl was carrying a tote bag decorated with a piano keyboard design.

She must be returning from piano class. As they headed towards the elevator, I heard the mother saying, 'You practised a lot, so you did very well today!'

I continued down the hall towards my first-floor unit.

Those were good memories.

In kindergarten, I used to go to an English conversation school, carrying a tote bag just like that. Instead of a keyboard design, my tote had 'Hello English' printed on it.

I couldn't remember whether my mother coaxed me into going or if I asked to go.

The conversation school, located in a room within a mixed-use building, held classes with only five students per group, taught by a Canadian teacher named Alec. He was an easy-going and cheerful man. I really liked Alec.

We learned to pronounce words first before learning to spell them. Alec gave us opportunities to chat and have fun, and we talked and sang using the English we learned by ear.

Sometimes, we gathered around a low table, and other times, we pushed it to the corner of the room to make space.

Alec, a gym rat, would flex his arm muscles, and we would hang from those burly arms, laughing and squealing in delight. Despite his knobby fingers, he would pat our heads and hold our hands tenderly as if we were something truly precious.

Alec couldn't speak Japanese. In hindsight, that might have been a lie. Maybe it was something he just let us believe. So, I had to speak English to communicate with Alec and pay close attention if I wanted to understand him.

I made a conscious effort to communicate with him, stringing together the few English words I knew. He was always incredibly positive, responding to everything I said like it was deeply impressive, his eyes twinkling.

He treated everyone equally. If one kid goofed off and interrupted another kid, he would get upset. And he always took the opportunity to hug each of us, saying, 'Everyone is so amazing! You, and you, and you, too!'

After a year, Alec moved back to Canada.

When I started grade school, instead of continuing at the kids' conversation school, I enrolled in an English school for elementary and junior high school students. When I told my mother that I wanted to keep learning English, she found the school in the neighbourhood.

Simply put, it was a cram school. The room was filled with desks and chairs, and Japanese teachers taught in front of a whiteboard.

In every class, there was a quiz. We were instructed to memorize the vocabulary from the textbook, and were told in advance which words would be on the quiz.

That's easy, I thought.

It was nothing compared to the times I'd racked my brain to figure out how to communicate with Alec. I only needed to memorize the words in front of me.

I earned a perfect score on every quiz. The teacher even complimented me on my pronunciation, which I'd picked up from Alec.

But instead of Alec, it was my mother who said, 'Good job, Kanato! You must have tried very hard!'

Hearing that made me happy. That was why I learned every word, mastered every grammar rule and achieved good results in speech contests.

Just so I could see my mother's happy face when she praised me.

~

The next day, in second-period math class, we got our final exam back. A 46. The average was 52. The score no longer shocked me. It was the mark of an inferior student, thrust in front of my face.

In fifth period, we got our geography exam back. The score written on mine was 57.

'The class average was sixty-four,' said Mr Yashiro.

Thank goodness. At least, I'd managed to avoid completely bombing in math and geography.

Despite my relief, I couldn't help but cringe about how anxious I had been about whether I passed or failed.

How far you have fallen, Kanato Miyahara.

'There were quite a few questions on the exam,' said Mr Yashiro. 'But this pales in comparison to the university entrance exams, so consider it practice.'

Practice for the university entrance exams.

Since he put it that way, I guessed it must be true. I didn't even question it.

Only recently, I had been studying for the high school entrance exams, and now I was expected to prepare for the university ones.

I wasn't sure if I wanted to go to university anymore. What was I studying for anyway?

26

Picking up a piece of chalk, Mr Yashiro turned his back to the class.

He wrote the scores of the top three students on the board:

1st: 97
2nd: 96
3rd: 88

The students' names weren't disclosed, so only the top three students knew their rankings. All the rest of us knew was that we had some pretty impressive students in our class.

In junior high, I used to be one of them.

But that was in the past, and I had chosen a small, ruthless world that I wasn't cut out for.

From now on, I'll live according to my current standing, doing just enough to avoid failing or flunking out.

Thinking this made me feel a bit better.

Maybe I'll work part-time. Shizukuda-san said she enjoyed working at the okonomiyaki place, and lots of burger shops and convenience stores are hiring.

Maybe it wouldn't be so bad to enjoy high school life a bit more.

Maybe being good at school isn't the be-all and end-all of life.

If I had a friend like Shizukuda-san, I might be able to enjoy myself more, and I could relax into a more laid-back school life as an underachiever.

Mr Yashiro's voice echoed in my mind. On the days we got our exam results, we would always go over the correct answers.

While the teacher explained the correct answers, I wrote them down in blue pen, filling in the spaces next to the wrong answers and in the blank areas where I hadn't written anything.

Toward the end of class, I noticed Shizukuda-san approaching the teacher at the lectern.

She spoke to Mr Yashiro in a whisper.

'You're an honest one.' Mr Yashiro chuckled, writing something down with a red pen.

He then turned to the chalkboard and made a correction with the eraser and chalk:

1st: 96
2nd: 95
3rd: 88

Huh? I almost gasped out loud.

Shizukuda-san quietly returned to her seat.

I understood immediately.

One of her wrong answers had been marked as correct, giving her two extra points. She reported the mistake to Mr Yashiro, so her score dropped from 97 to 95.

It was likely that everyone in the class, not just me, realized: Shizukuda-san had come second in the geography exam.

～

After school, Shizukuda-san approached me at my desk.

'Did you bring *Bura-man*?' she asked with a sunny expression.

I couldn't look her in the eyes.

I handed her a shopping bag with five books inside. I couldn't smile or talk to her the way I had at the park.

Taking the manga from me, she tilted her head slightly. 'Is something wrong?'

'Er, no . . .' I said, forcing a smile. 'I didn't know you were smart.'

She stared at me, disbelief written all over her face, as my words spilled out, dripping with sarcasm.

'A ninety-five is amazing. If you hadn't said anything, you would've been first.'

'Oh, that,' she said bluntly, and my anger flared.

Admit it, you were only pretending to be bad at school when you're actually not. Were you just messing with me?

Some people are like that, I guess. They act like they're goofing off to lower your guard, but in reality, they're getting top grades.

'I thought you said you were horrible at geography.' I couldn't keep from snapping at her.

'I am,' she replied matter-of-factly. 'I *am* horrible at it. That's why I had to study really, really hard.'

Her eyes pierced right through me.

She continued, 'It wasn't that I wanted to beat anyone. I just wanted to do my best.'

Her words floored me.

I stared at Shizukuda-san, speechless.

Her eyes flitted away from mine as she said, 'I'll see you,' without waiting for a response, then turned and walked away.

My chest throbbed with pain as I stood there, dazed and unmoving.

~

My steps were heavy as I walked to the park.

Since I had no one to vent to, I just wanted to be in Kabahiko's comforting presence. I wanted to pray for the smart version of me to come back.

The image of Shizukuda-san's back as she walked away from our conversation was burned into my mind and wouldn't go away. She probably wasn't interested in talking to me anymore. Given the harsh words, it was understandable. Still, it was a tough pill to swallow. As I kept walking, sweat began to bead on my skin. It was an especially muggy day, even for mid-July.

I felt thirsty. Spotting the awning of Sunrise Cleaning up ahead, I made a beeline for the vending machine.

I inserted two hundred-yen coins in the slot and pressed the button for Calpico Water. The bottle fell into the dispenser with a thud, along with the pleasant clinking of coins.

'Hey?'

The Calpico Water cost one hundred and fifty yen, but when I stuck my finger in the coin cup, there were two coins inside.

The previous person must have forgotten their change. I placed the coins in my palms.

Score!

No one would notice if I slipped the coins in my wallet. Fifty yen was a small enough sum that the owner wouldn't be inconvenienced or hurt by the loss.

As I went to open my wallet, I thought of Shizukuda-san.

She had reported that her 97 was really a 95.

Had she not said anything, none of us would have known.

She could have stayed in the top spot.

It wasn't that I wanted to beat anyone. I just wanted to do my best.

'How do I compete with that?' I muttered out loud.

I dropped one fifty-yen coin in my wallet and closed my hand around the other.

I grabbed the bottle with my free hand and drank the Calpico Water in big gulps. After some thought,

I peered through the glass storefront of Sunrise Cleaning.

An elderly woman sat at the counter, almost buried in piles of clothes in plastic wrap. Her silver-streaked hair was styled neatly in a short cut. She might be the woman Shizukuda-san had mentioned, the one whose herniated disk was healed after she rubbed Kabahiko's back.

I opened the door, and the woman looked up.

'Excuse me, someone forgot their change in the vending machine out front.'

I held out the fifty-yen coin. She let out an astonished croak. 'Do you go to school with Mifuyu-chan?'

'Huh?'

'Mifuyu Shizukuda.'

She tapped on her collarbone a few times. She seemed to be referring to the school insignia on my shirt.

'Oh . . . yes.'

'The Shizukudas have been regular customers for years. She's a good kid, that Mifuyu-chan.'

'Er . . . yeah.'

'She keeping busy at her part-time job?'

'I think so.'

It looked like the conversation might drag on. Just as I tuned out and tried to leave, she put away the fifty-yen coin in a drawer. 'Did you know she has six brothers and sisters?'

Six?

I had no idea she came from such a large family.

'She has her heart set on making enough to cover her high school expenses, which is admirable. But she doesn't want her grades to suffer as a result, so she studies hard. Considering she doesn't even have a room to herself, I'd say she's doing a heck of a job.'

I felt like I'd been punched in the gut.

She sounds a little too perfect . . .

A swirl of emotions mixed together into a tangled mess: feelings of respect and jealousy for Shizukuda-san, frustration with myself, and a sense of defensiveness.

The door opened, and in walked a woman with her hair gathered into a braid, carrying a large shopping bag. The elderly woman greeted her with a hearty 'Welcome'.

I quietly left the shop.

I couldn't bring myself to ask Kabahiko so casually to repair my brain anymore. I turned back up the path that I'd come down, and instead of heading to the park, I went home.

~

After opening the door to an empty apartment, I kicked off my shoes. On the dining room table was a note:

Heat the curry and enjoy. There's salad in the fridge.

That's right. Mom went to see a play with her friends.
I let out a huge sigh of relief.
At least I'll be spared from having to tell her about the exams today.
After changing into some lounge wear, I lost myself playing a battle game on my smartphone. I took down enemies and racked up points, cursing under my breath as I mashed my fingers on the screen.

As day turned to night and I grew hungry, I ate the curry and salad, then flopped on the sofa.
I'm tired. I wish something exciting would happen.
I closed my eyes and became sleepy. Wavering

between wakefulness and sleep, I thought of the boy deep in the mountains. *How great would it be if all he wanted to do was run for the sake of running? What did I want to do? I wish someone would tell me.*

Before I knew it, I was drawn into a deep sleep. When I woke up, I found my father sitting at the dining table. It seemed I had slept for two hours before realizing he had come home.

'You're home,' I said, rubbing the sleep from my eyes.

'Hey, you were sleeping well.'

I noticed the blanket draped over my shoulders. My father must have put it there.

'Did you eat dinner?' he asked.

'Yeah, how about you?'

'Yeah.'

My father sat hunched over the table, focusing intently on a task. I got up from the sofa and moved closer. He was writing something in permanent marker on some gardening labels shaped like birds and squirrels.

'What are those?' I asked.

'They're cute, huh? I found them at the hundred–

yen shop,' my father responded happily. 'They're plant labels for the garden.'

Zinnias. Begonias. Duranta.

They appeared to be names of flowers, though I couldn't imagine from the names what they might look like.

Thinking it would be awkward to retreat to my room, I picked up the TV remote. I found a variety show that my father also liked and sat back down on the sofa.

It was a talk show that was MC'ed by a big-name personality. A young comedian was doing his best to impress the MC with a funny story.

'I have a Pachira plant at home that understands everything I say! If I tell it to grow that way, its branches grow that way. If I tell it, "Good job" or "Well done", its leaves become glossy.'

The famous MC quipped, 'That plant's smarter than you are.'

My father chuckled.

I asked, 'Do you do stuff like that?'

'Stuff like what?'

'People say that you can help a plant's growth by

saying how beautiful it is and praising it. You don't do that?'

Indirectly, I was asking a question that had always lingered in my mind.

My father was always kind, yet he hardly ever praised me about anything. This was always a source of mystery and worry. Maybe, in his heart of hearts, he was just cold.

My father shook his head. 'No, not me.'

That's what I thought.

He couldn't be moved to praise even the plants he doted on.

I muttered, 'Well, it's not like the flowers can understand you, so . . .' and went back to watching TV. I didn't want to dig deeper and risk getting hurt.

After a while, my father continued, 'I'm not questioning whether plants can understand. It's just the opposite. I believe they *can* understand what we say. That's why words come with responsibility.'

I shifted my gaze towards him.

Picking up a bird-shaped label, he continued, 'Working hard for praise isn't necessarily a bad thing. But if that's your only motivation, you're likely to feel defeated when that praise doesn't come.'

I felt a sudden twinge in my heart.

My father seemed to be indirectly answering the question that had been lingering in my mind.

Gently yet firmly, he said, 'So you weren't praised. So what? Regardless of what anyone says or doesn't say, flowers will always do their best to bloom.'

He looked me in the eyes and smiled.

'That's why all I have to do is love them. That's all.'

With that, he went back to writing on the labels.

I clutched the blanket on the sofa, on the verge of tears.

My father's love was exactly like the blanket. It was that gentle softness of the cotton fabric being placed over me, as I slept, defenceless. I should have known better, but I could never truly be certain until now.

I recalled Alec's words:

Everyone is so amazing. You, and you, and you, too!
Oh, that's right. Now I understand.

Alec wasn't just praising us.

He also loved us. And as children, we felt his love with our whole bodies.

'Whoops,' my father said softly.

I glanced over and saw a black line dashed across the edge of the table.

The table was a Scandinavian piece my mother adored and had splurged on even though it was over budget. The edge was randomly inlaid with tiles of various colours, and it looked like the pen had rolled away, smearing ink on a white tile.

'Your mum is going to be upset with me.' He rose to his feet without any hint of trepidation.

As I waited anxiously to see what he would do next, he went into the bathroom and came out almost immediately.

In his hand was a tube of toothpaste.

Humming cheerfully, he applied the toothpaste over the black line and rubbed it gently with a paper towel.

No way. I watched the scene in anticipation.

When he finished wiping away the toothpaste, he grinned.

I looked at the spot where the ink used to be and gasped.

It was gone!

~

The next morning, I headed straight for Hinode Park.

Perhaps because it was still early on a Saturday morning, there were few people out. The playground was even more deserted than usual.

'Kabahiko!'

I called the hippo by name, just as Shizukuda-san had that day.

Although he couldn't possibly answer, he looked right at me. At least, he seemed to.

I rubbed my hands all over Kabahiko's head.

There, there. Good boy.

Hang on, I'll clean you right up.

I swung one leg over the hippo and sat on it.

From my knapsack, I took out a pack of tissues and a toothbrush kit, which I found in the bathroom drawer.

I squeezed the toothpaste from the tiny tube on to the first letters written on Kabahiko's head. I scrubbed nervously with the toothbrush.

'Yes!'

I broke into a smile.

The black ink was gone, revealing Kabahiko's dull orange hue underneath. Trying to contain my excitement, I squeezed the toothpaste on to the remaining letters and worked the brush over them, careful not to apply too much pressure.

Gone.

The letters spelling out 'stupid' had disappeared!

After wiping away every last bit of toothpaste with a tissue, I shouted, 'Yes!' even louder this time.

I won't let anyone call you stupid ever again.

I wished I could share this triumph with Shizukuda-san. In the next instant, I felt my heart sinking.

She probably hates me now.

I glanced at the swings and recalled her sitting on one, pumping her legs enthusiastically, her cheeks flushed.

Decompress and recharge.

Those were the ways she regulated and righted herself.

She must have studied harder than I could ever imagine, all while caring for her family and others around her.

And me? All I did was sulk without putting in any real effort.

Telling myself I wasn't stupid. That I was better than this.

How embarrassing! I mean, seriously!

What needed fixing was my self-pitying and arrogance.

I used to work so hard just to talk to Alec; I used to enjoy English so much. All I wanted back then was to learn.

I gently rubbed Kabahiko's head.

Please, Kabahiko.

Please help me heal my twisted, stubborn head.

Straddling Kabahiko, I wrapped both my arms around his head and rested my cheek against it.

The rounded back of Kabahiko's head, fragrant with mint, felt good and cool against my skin.

When I got home, I collected all the returned exams and took them into the living room.

My mother was running the vacuum cleaner while my father was out in the garden.

As soon as she turned off the vacuum, I called out to her, and she turned towards me.

'I have something to tell you. Is now a good time?'

Her expression turned tense. 'What is it?' with a nervous smile, she asked.

I laid out the exams side by side on the table.

Forty-six in math. Fifty-seven in geography.

'The average scores were fifty-six in math and sixty-four in geography.'

'What?'

My mother stuck out her neck slightly, looking more surprised than angry.

'I didn't even get the average score. Because of my lack of effort.'

Then there was the English exam with the 89 written on it.

As my mother watched, I drew two lines through the number with a red pen.

'I'm sorry—I lied. I altered the score.'

Her eyes widened.

I ran the red pen across the blank space next to it: 61.

Fixed it.

Now, this was a true healing.

I handed my mother the exam.

'This is my real score.'

With the exam in her hand, she looked alternately at the score and me, seemingly at a loss for words.

'I misunderstood. I thought I was smart—that I could do well without even trying.'

But that wasn't the case.

Up until I passed the recommendation-based admissions exam, I had diligently done everything I needed to do.

But after that, I became complacent. While everyone else was studying their hardest, I was lazing around doing nothing.

Now, well into my new life in high school, I still hadn't done anything.

I had yet to study properly, think about my future or make friends.

Or put in the effort necessary to succeed at the school I had got into.

'I'm going to try my best from now on.'

It wasn't about winning or losing. It was about putting in my best effort.

My mother's cheeks softened into a smile. 'It's not about the results, Kanato. What makes me happy is seeing you putting in the effort.'

Suddenly, I felt a warmth come over me, remembering how my mother always told me, 'You must have tried very hard!'

My father poked his head in from the garden.

'The dahlias have bloomed. Come have a look,' he said, a huge smile spread across his face.

We went out into the garden.

The freshly bloomed dahlias had opened their petals, surely nourished by my father's care.

Loving them with all his heart.

~

The moment I stepped into the classroom on Monday morning, Shizukuda-san ran up to me as if she had been waiting for my arrival.

'Miyahara-kun! The *Bura-man* you lent me was amazing!' she said, holding up one of the volumes in her hand.

With my mouth half open, I watched her rattle off like a machine gun. As Shizukuda-san gushed about the best parts of the story and which characters were her favourite, I nodded along, and felt my worries and regrets melt away.

She was her usual self. Letting out a sigh of relief, I said, 'I thought you hated me.'

Shizukuda-san blinked at me with a puzzled expression.

'Huh? Why?'

'You left without hardly talking to me on Friday.'

'What? I was just in a hurry to go to work.'

Ah, she must have looked away from me to check the clock.

'Still, I said all that awful stuff to you and . . . and I was horrible because I was jealous of you doing your best. I'm sorry.'

'Oh? Is that what you thought? I wouldn't hate you for something like that.'

Shizukuda-san cackled, giving me a light pat on the arm.

'You're so stupid!'

Her voice sounded so warm that I got a little teary-eyed.

Yeah, I really was stupid.

2

Sawa's Mouth

'Thank you.'

How many times in a day had I said those words before?

Thank you. Thank you.

Every time the words left my mouth, my heart overflowed with gratitude and pride.

'Sawa-chan, Mizuho-chan's forehead is sweaty. I'll wipe it for her,' offered Akemi-san, a mum friend, with a thin smile as the children filed out of the bus at the designated stop. Before I could respond, she pressed a rumpled gauze handkerchief to my daughter Mizuho's face.

It was three o'clock on a September day after summer break, and the sun was still blazing. The bus, muggy with the heat of the excited children, must have been too hot for sweaty Mizuho.

'Ew, her hands are sticky. Let me wipe them for her, so she doesn't get it on the other kids,' Akemi-san added.

'Th-thanks,' I answered, fumbling to pull out my handkerchief. *Too late.*

There wasn't a hint of pride or gratitude in that thank-you.

Only cowering regret.

⁓

Last year, my husband Yoshitaka had suggested buying a condominium.

I was rather fond of the two-bedroom apartment we'd lived in until then and was hesitant about the restrictions of home ownership. For one thing, if something were to happen, it wouldn't be so easy to move. Besides, the thought of being saddled with years of loans put me off.

'There's a nice property near the station,' said Yoshitaka. 'My parents said they'll help with the down payment.'

He handed me a full-colour flyer as if he'd already made up his mind. Although I knew he had spoken to his mother before mentioning it to me, I couldn't voice my dissatisfaction. I wasn't earning a single yen at the time.

Advance Hill. The flyer didn't include a real photo of the condominium, just a computer-generated image—a glittering idealized version.

It wasn't just the shiny condominium. The sky was a perfect blue, and the surrounding trees were lush with vibrant greens. Though I knew it was just a dream, I nearly succumbed to the illusion that this home—and the entire world—could be ours.

On a day off, Yoshitaka, Mizuho and I visited a pop-up model room set up near the train station.

From the living room to the kitchen and the bathroom, everything seemed as if a future life had been prepared for us, even though none of it was real, and no one actually lived there. Mizuho squealed excitedly at the polka-dot curtains and the large bathtub.

The sales representative, following closely behind us, extolled the charms of the condominium, spraying spittle as he spoke. On the wall of the meeting space hung a layout chart of the five-storey building, with red paper flowers stuck to several of the squares.

An older couple and their adult daughter were standing by the chart. Moments later, another sales representative came in and stuck a flower on a space on the third floor. Seemingly having closed the deal, the sales rep bowed deeply towards the family.

Yoshitaka waited for them to leave before examining the layout chart.

'Hey, this one seems nice,' he said, pointing to a three-bedroom unit on the second floor not yet claimed by a flower. 'If we're on the second floor, even if the elevator isn't working, we won't be too inconvenienced. Plus, the price point is . . .'

The price was certainly more reasonable than that of a four-bedroom unit on the upper floors. But what about the sunlight? The noise pollution? The smells? We'd only come today to see the model room. We needed to visit the construction site too, and check out the surrounding area first.

Another concern was where Mizuho would attend kindergarten. By the time the condominium was completed in spring, she would be six. Changing schools at such a crucial age would be tough on her.

Just as I was about to suggest going home to think it over, the sales rep, who had overheard Yoshitaka, chimed in, 'There was a customer in here earlier who was considering purchasing this unit. Just say the word, and I'll hold it for you.'

My husband's face lit up. As he moved to sit down at the sales rep's urging, I tugged on his sleeve and whispered, 'What about Mizuho's kindergarten?'

'That's no problem. Kids adapt.'

'But . . .'

He leaned in closer to Mizuho, and said, 'You want to live in a new house, too, don't you?'

The girl threw up her hands. 'Yay!'

'See? A property like this doesn't come around every day. We shouldn't let it slip away.'

He turned to the salesman and signed the contract right then and there.

～

And so, the matter of our moving was quickly settled, and I found myself running around with all sorts of paperwork and preparations.

Of them, finding a kindergarten for Mizuho and arranging her transfer was the most concerning. Unable to find a school within walking distance that would accept her, I contacted several schools with bus routes near our condominium.

Eventually, we settled on Hibari Kindergarten. Unlike the cosy, tight-knit vibe of the previous school, the new one was much larger and had rather nitpicky regulations. For starters, Mizuho's tote bag and shoe bag had to be handmade, and the items in the tool case she'd always used didn't meet regulations.

When the day finally arrived, Mizuho, who didn't fully understand what transferring meant, cried inconsolably. My heart broke watching her, and all I could do was hold her.

But three days later, I was relieved to see her laughing with her new friends. Yoshitaka had been right. Kids do adapt.

And me?

I let out a quiet sigh and glanced at the wall clock. It was 7.15 a.m.

'Time to go, Mizuho. Hurry up, or we're going to miss the bus!'

I plopped her school cap on to her head while she ignored me, absorbed in a picture book. I checked my modestly made-up face in the mirror and grabbed my tote bag.

The designated bus stop for the neighbourhood was the roundabout in front of the supermarket, Murray's.

Every weekday morning and afternoon, the same groups of parents gathered to drop off and pick up their children. Of the ten or so parents gathered there, several had children around Mizuho's age, so naturally, I ended up joining that group.

At first, they called me 'Himura-san,' using my last name, but before long, I was being called by my first name—Sawa-chan—just like in my school days. It embarrassed me at first, but being the only one to continue calling the others by their last name felt a bit standoffish, so I decided to follow suit.

So, Maejima-san became 'Fumie-chan', and

Yukimura-san became 'Kaho-chan'. Only Nishimoto-san, the leader of the mum group, was given the polite honorific—Akemi-san, so I did the same. Fumie-chan was thirty-five, like me, and Kaho-chan was thirty-seven, but Akemi-san was in her mid-forties. Anri-chan had an older brother in the sixth grade, so Akemi-san had been a mother for longer than the rest of us.

As I led Mizuho by the hand towards the round-about, the mothers were all chatting in a circle while the children jumped around.

'Here's Sawa-chan.'

Akemi-san waved at me, and I waved back. Fumie-chan and Kaho-chan glanced at me long enough to smile, then returned to gossiping about something I couldn't follow. I stood there with an awkward smile, feeling a little out of place.

Six months had passed since we first moved, back in April, but I still felt anxious about fitting into this established group. The previous kindergarten had been a five-minute walk from home, so I hadn't had to see the same people at the same time every day. Although I did socialize with some mum friends back then, they all seemed much more laid back.

With Mizuho's graduation only six months away, I told myself I had to make it work somehow. As long as I went along with the others and kept a low profile, I couldn't be left out. I made an effort to maintain a pleasant, comfortable distance.

'Look, Mizuho-chan!'

Anri-chan pointed to the keychain on her school bag. It was a keychain of an anime character Mizuho liked.

'Ooh, that's nice!'

Letting go of my hand, Mizuho padded up to Anri-chan. The moment they met, the two had become fast friends. Honestly, I was grateful to have Anri-chan around.

'Did you get the coupon?' Akemi-san asked.

Fumie-chan pulled out her cell phone. 'Yep, got it! So, should we all do the Samantha?'

'Let's go!' said Kaho-san.

I immediately understood they were talking about the app-exclusive discount coupon for the fast-food place, Samantha, inside Murray's supermarket.

After sending the children off on the morning bus, the mums usually spent the morning chatting at Samantha until it was time to pick them up. They called this activity 'doing the Samantha'.

'You're coming too, right, Sawa-chan?' Akemi-san turned to me.

In an instant, all sorts of excuses swirled through my head:

I've got other plans today. I left the house with the washing machine running. I have a bit of a headache.

But instead, I found myself saying, 'Sure, I'll go.'

It would have been awkward to make up an excuse and risk getting called out on a lie—especially if it really was a lie.

Just then, a mother named Kinugawa-san arrived at the bus stop, holding hands with her son, Tomoki-kun.

'Good morning,' she said, her long, black hair swaying. The other mothers nodded in response.

Kinugawa-san was another mother with a six-year-old in kindergarten.

However, the other mothers treated her like a nuisance. She had a slender frame, always carried herself straight, and seemed quite taciturn. I'd never seen her smiling or engaging in conversation with anyone. Her son, Tomoki-kun, was also quiet and rarely spoke to the other kids. Though we seemed to be around the same age, I found her unapproachable and kept my distance.

The school bus arrived, and the children climbed aboard.

Then, Kinugawa-san gave a clipped 'Excuse me' and left.

The four of us mum friends hung out at Samantha, using the store app's discount coupon. Akemi-san said, 'We should have a meeting about the bazaar sometime next week or the week after next.'

This year, I was on the bazaar committee, a role I wasn't too keen on. At the principal's express wishes, a fundraising bazaar was being held for the first time at Hibari Kindergarten. Every parent was expected to take on a role each year, and although I had planned to join the beautification committee, which involved periodic cleaning and weeding of the school grounds, Akemi-san had goaded me into joining the bazaar committee instead.

'Committees are such a bore. We might as well have fun together. Come on.' I couldn't refuse.

While I could do the cleaning and weeding quietly by myself, an event like this required lots of group cooperation and planning.

With the bazaar scheduled for November, it was already about time to start planning. With a heavy heart, I opened my planner, which barely had any appointments.

Akemi-san, who was the leader of the mothers of the six-year-old class, said with a hint of annoyance, 'Well, I suppose the four of us can use our group chat, and the parents of the other age groups can do the same. Oh, wait, we need to contact Kinugawa-san.'

Kinugawa-san was also on the bazaar committee. In her case, she had volunteered rather than been invited.

'Isn't she busy with work?' Kaho-chan said dismissively. There had been a time when Kaho-chan had invited Kinugawa-san to Samantha, but she had flatly refused the invitation due to work. Kaho-chan hadn't invited her since, clearly peeved by her response.

'What does she do for a living anyway?' asked Akemi-san.

Kaho-chan shrugged.

'Who knows? I think she sometimes works in extended daycare.'

'I don't think I've ever even seen her husband,' added Fumie-chan. 'She's a complete mystery.'

Akemi-san sipped her melon soda and leaned forward. 'Tomoki-kun is unusually quiet, don't you think? He hardly talks and makes no effort to fit in. I don't know how he'll manage in this world.'

Tomoki-kun certainly didn't strike me as the type to romp around outside. On music recital days, while the other kids were making a ruckus after the performance, he was in a corner by himself folding origami.

Afterward, the mothers let rip with speculations about Kinugawa-san—whether she was divorced, involved in some shady business, if she looked down on them, and so on.

Over the past six months, I thought I'd gotten pretty good at nodding along. The key was not to disagree with anything anyone said. I simply reacted with 'Really?' or 'Wow, is that right?' feigning ignorance, while occasionally adding 'No way!' or 'Gosh!'

'*Hmph*, does she think she's better than us just

because she works?' Akemi-san said, furrowing her brows. Something deep inside me creaked uncomfortably at her words.

~

'Welcome! How can I help you?'

On Saturday afternoon while my husband was out at work, I was sitting down on the sofa after washing the dishes when Mizuho called out a greeting.

She waved me over from behind a makeshift display case fashioned out of an overturned cardboard box. Lately, playing store had become her favourite activity.

The box had a grid drawn on it with marker, and inside each square, she had arranged different items into various self-made categories. Today, the store appeared to be a sticker shop.

A freebie sticker of an anime character from a magazine, a sweepstakes ticket stuck to a bread bag, a decorative sticker on a box of candy, and office labels that she must have found in a drawer. Having gathered stickers from all around the house, she had stuck some on to memo paper and placed sheets of unused ones for sale at her shop.

Since Mizuho always wanted to play the store clerk, I took on the role of customer.

I picked up a sticker of a bird between my fingers.

'This is lovely.'

Standing on the other side of the cardboard box, Mizuho nodded enthusiastically.

'Yes, it's a special sticker from overseas.'

'Oh, I see,' I said, playing along. 'Where is it from?'

'It's from a magical kingdom.'

'*Wow*. How much is it?'

'Um . . . eight hundred yen.'

'That's a bit expensive.'

'That's because when you wear the sticker, you can fly like a bird.'

'What? In that case, I'll take it!'

'Great! I'll wrap it up for you.'

Her polite language was a bit clumsy, but for an impromptu performance, her customer service was quite impressive.

With Mizuho absorbed in her role as a shop

clerk, I smiled at her precocious mannerisms and found myself reminiscing.

~

Before I became pregnant, I used to work at Ainé.

It was a national retail chain with outlets typically located at train stations. After graduating from junior college, I started working at a women's clothing store.

Ainé had a system where sales staff with excellent customer service skills were recognized as fashion ambassadors known as 'Ainests'. Unlike the silver name badge typically worn by regular staff, Ainests were distinguished by black badges, although this was not widely known to customers.

Once a year, a national competition was held where approximately thirty thousand Ainests from across the country gathered to compete in a role-playing contest, showcasing their superior customer service skills. After less than two years on the job, I began wearing a black badge on my chest and even won a special award at the national competition.

I enjoyed working in customer service and took pride in greeting customers with a smile and a thank-you. Answering their questions, making fashion recommendations, and interacting with them were things I'd truly enjoyed.

Yet now, I found myself struggling to talk to my mum friends.

Just what was I supposed to say?

'Thank you for waiting.'

Mizuho held out the bird sticker, now wrapped in tissue. I pretended to hand her payment, which she accepted with both hands.

Money that was invisible to the eye now rested in Mizuho's hands. Though it wasn't actually there, she could see it as if it were. Anything was possible in the world of make-believe. This sticker would allow me to fly like a bird.

Just as Mizuho was playing shop, perhaps I was also playing at being a mum friend. I didn't consider any of them my friends at all.

I was living in a fake world, like the computer-generated ad for Advance Hill, merely acting the part of a mum friend.

That would have been fine if I actually enjoyed it. But now, I was just trying to get through this unwanted role until the performance was over.

'Thank you.'

Mizuho bowed her small head and smiled in satisfaction.

~

In the evening, as I was heading out to go shopping, my cell phone rang.

The call was from my mother, who lived some distance away.

Mizuho and I were already on our way. I turned off the busy street to take the call.

'Hello?'

'Hi, it's me. Everything alright?'

'Yeah, Mum.'

Listening to my mother's unhurried voice, I guided Mizuho with my free hand down a backstreet. We then walked into a residential neighbourhood and towards an apartment complex. I had recently discovered a tiny park tucked away among the buildings.

As my mother chatted, Mizuho and I made our way into the park marked by a stone slab at the entrance that read 'Hinode Park'.

Mizuho made a dash for the swings and began pumping her legs back and forth.

It didn't seem like my mother's rambling would end anytime soon.

I took a seat on one of the animal rides, a hippo with peeling orange paint. Its expression was so relaxed and free of any tension that you couldn't tell whether it was smiling or crying.

'Will red be all right for Mizuho's school backpack? I went to the department store the other day and was shocked at how expensive they are.'

She had wanted to buy a new school backpack for Mizuho to celebrate starting elementary school next year. She lived in the countryside about five hours by bullet train from Tokyo, so we only saw her once or twice a year.

After we moved to Advance Hill, we had invited both my in-laws and my own parents over separately. We were able to see Yoshitaka's parents more often than mine, since they lived in Tokyo.

'Red would be great, Mum. Thanks.'

I imagined my mother, who relied on her pension, shopping for backpacks at the department store, and a warm feeling filled my chest. She was still healthy and still thinking about her family.

Had she lived closer, I might have carried on working at the shop. After Mizuho was born, I went back to working at Ainé.

But things didn't work out as planned. The daycare was closed on Sundays and holidays, and I couldn't align my days off with the daycare's schedule. Plus, Yoshitaka frequently had to work on weekends at the clothing company. We agreed that Yoshitaka's mother would take care of Mizuho, but as much as she loved her granddaughter, caring for a baby proved to be too much for her.

After two months, she said, 'Sawa-san, perhaps a child should be with her mother at least until she turns three.'

Yoshitaka didn't exactly disagree with that opinion.

That wasn't all. Mizuho was often feverish, which led to regular calls from the daycare. Each time, I had to leave work early, and I could only imagine the trouble I must have caused for the staff. If that wasn't enough, my health began to suffer from a lack of sleep and exhaustion. I started making small mistakes and became forgetful. Feeling exhausted, I couldn't provide the level of customer service I strived for, and it was weighing on me.

And so I quit my job.

I didn't regret my decision. It felt far better to be able to watch Mizuho grow up, even if I had to care for her on my own rather than to have to shamefully ask my mother-in-law for childcare favours.

At least until she turns three.

I had agreed and stepped away from work. But even after Mizuho turned four, and then five, I still hadn't gone back. I'd considered finding a job once she started kindergarten, but I couldn't make up my mind. Whether she was a newborn or a toddler, she was still my child. I no longer felt confident that I could return to work and make up for lost time in the workplace or even manage that kind of life again.

'How is Yoshitaka-san? Busy with work as usual?' my mother asked.

'Uh huh,' I managed in reply.

'I hope you're grateful that he got you such a nice new condominium,' she continued cheerfully.

I paused. Wait, Yoshitaka *got me* a condominium?

Did I have to thank him for it?

My mother was a kind woman, certainly, but she lacked empathy. She would never understand the inner turmoil I was feeling.

Just then, Mizuho hopped off the swing and scampered over to me. I handed her the phone so she could spend a few minutes talking to her grandmother before I ended the call.

The closest supermarket to Advance Hill was the Asahi Store. Although it was smaller than Murray's, its compactly organized shelves made it easy to find what I needed.

I loaded the cart with several days' worth of groceries and household goods, allowed Mizuho to choose one of the snacks she was begging for, and headed to the register.

I scanned the faces of the cashiers at each register and chose a line. There was one cashier whose customer service skills were impeccable. No matter how busy her line was, I always sought her out because she made the shopping experience so pleasurable.

She was probably around fifty years old or so. She always radiated joy, as though even the crow's feet around her eyes were a stamp of her happiness.

She wore a dark green polo shirt, which was the Asahi Store's uniform. I had noticed the name 'Shizukuda' on her name badge early on. Shizukuda-san. In my heart, she was my Ainest.

Her care in handling each item was impressive. I watched, captivated, as she placed each item into a basket like perfect puzzle pieces.

After ringing up the groceries, she leaned down slightly to meet Mizuho's eyeline.

'Can I scan that for you?'

Mizuho held up her snack.

Shizukuda-san placed the scanner against the barcode on the box and said, 'Pip!' Mizuho giggled. She cut off a strip of tape in the store's colours and stuck it across the box.

From asking for a points card to handing back change, every action was smooth and efficient, leaving nothing to be desired.

'Thank you.' Shizukuda-san looked me in the eyes with a charming smile.

As we took our basket to the bagging counter,

Mizuho stared at the tape stuck to her snack as proof of purchase. It would likely become a sales item in her sticker store—another successful acquisition.

'Shizukuda-san gave you a nice one!' I said, packing everything into a tote bag.

'Shizukuda-san?'

'The name of the nice lady at the cash register. Her name was on the badge on her chest.'

'Oh!'

Mizuho's innocent reaction made me smile.

'Did you know I used to sell clothes wearing a badge like that a long time ago?'

'*Really?*' Mizuho's eyes lit up.

It was the first time I'd told her. Until now, I hadn't been able to bring myself to say it.

Mizuho responded eagerly, 'If you wear a badge, everyone will know who you are!'

'That's right!' I chuckled, then absent-mindedly glanced at a corner of the now-empty cart.

Now that I no longer had a name badge, *who was I?*

≈

Around four o'clock the following Monday, Akemi-san and I met at the train station along with our daughters.

The only silver lining about moving was that I had found a good piano school nearby. Located inside a community building near the station, the school offered group lessons at a reasonable monthly price. The teacher was kind and gentle, and Mizuho had quickly grown attached to her. She had been given a trial lesson and liked it, and so I emptied my secret savings to buy her a small, second-hand piano. Due to lack of space and sound-proofing, this wouldn't have been allowed in our previous rental.

It was true—no matter what the circumstances, there were always positives to be found.

But last week, when Akemi-san asked, 'Where is Mizuho-chan's piano school?' a dark cloud seemed to roll in.

'Anri wants to check out the school. Do you think we can observe one of Mizuho-chan's lessons?'

'Oh . . . sure. But they also offer trial lessons. Maybe she'd like that better,' I suggested quietly, but Akemi-san shook her head.

'She just wants to watch. If she decides she wants to give it a try, she can take a trial lesson then.'

It wasn't a request I could refuse.

I contacted the school to get permission for Anri-chan to observe a lesson.

And now, the four of us were on our way to the school.

Mizuho and Anri-chan walked side by side, like two peas in a pod, slightly ahead of us. Cheerful Anri-chan and chatty Mizuho never seemed to tire of talking to each other.

When we arrived outside the school, Akemi-san took a look at the building, 'Oh, is this it? I expected it to be bigger.'

What exactly had she been imagining? Today wasn't a recital day, and it wasn't unusual for a music school to be located inside a building.

'Welcome. You must be Anri-chan,' the teacher greeted warmly.

Akemi-san bowed her head. 'Nice to meet you.'

Throughout the lesson, Anri-chan swung her legs back and forth out of boredom while Mizuho kept glancing at her, distracted.

About five minutes before the lesson ended, the

teacher asked Anri-chan, 'Would you like to give it a try?'

Anri-chan happily hopped off her chair. The teacher moved the chair next to Mizuho, and Anri-chan took a seat and extended her arms.

The teacher guided her slowly, but Anri-chan was barely paying attention. She tapped random keys with her index finger, producing a series of ugly sounds that echoed loudly.

Kya ha ha ha!

Kya ha ha ha!

Anri-chan and Mizuho's laughter overlapped into a duet, filling the room.

I forced an uneasy smile, feeling a bit sorry for the teacher. Before long, the bell rang, and all I could do was pray that Anri-chan wouldn't ask her mother if she could start at the school.

Several days later, I received a message from Akemi-san on the group LINE chat.

Look what I found! This is you, right, Sawa-chan?

The link that she sent was for an online article about the time I participated in the Ainest competition years ago. My skin broke out in a clammy sweat.

There was a picture of me in my twenties, wearing a black badge, standing on the stage, holding up a special award plaque.

My full name, before I got married, also appeared in the article.

Wow, Sawa-chan.

You look beautiful!

We never knew!

The messages appeared on the phone screen in rapid succession.

Hastily, I scrambled for the right response.

It was painful to be praised for something I'd achieved so long ago, and I was terrified of what the other mums really thought.

It's nothing.

The moment I hit send, I wondered whether I had made a mistake in my choice of words. The number next to the read notification shot up instantly, but nobody responded.

Worry crept over me from the tips of my toes. What should I do? What—what should I say?

That was a long time ago.

I hastily followed up with a second message and a sticker of a silly, sweating face.

After a while, Akemi-san responded with a sticker of a dog clapping; then the chat screen went quiet.

As I anxiously made my way to the bus stop the next morning, Akemi-san called, 'Sawa-chan's here,' with a smile. Fumie-chan and Kaho-chan also chimed in with their usual greeting, and all the tension left my body.

Thank goodness. It didn't seem as serious as I had thought.

We exchanged the latest celebrity gossip until the bus arrived, and saw the children off to school.

As I considered the task of airing out the futons on this sunny day, Akemi-san asked, 'We were talking about doing the Samantha today. You'll come too, right, Sawa-chan?'

I couldn't bring myself to want to go. Still, I felt a tinge of relief for being asked. I wasn't being left out. Everything was fine.

Once inside Murray's, we ordered drinks from our usual table in the back. After chatting about the goings-on at the kindergarten, Akemi-san fixed me with a hard look.

'Listen, something's been on my mind, so I'll just say it.'

My body froze.

She continued steadily as if building up to something. 'It's about the piano school.'

The piano school? Not about the Ainest article from yesterday.

Akemi-san knotted her brows, her lips twisted to the side. She was smiling, but her eyes flashed.

'When Anri couldn't play the piano properly, Mizuho-chan started laughing at her.'

'*What?*' I nearly blurted out. I couldn't understand what she was talking about. Akemi-san's face contorted even more. 'It broke my heart, that's all. Mizuho-chan has been going for a while, so it's only natural she can play. But laughing at someone who was just starting out—I don't know . . . it just shocked me.'

If she felt this way, why couldn't she have told me so when the two of us were alone? Why did she have to bring it up in front of the others?

Fumie-chan and Kaho-chan stared at me, their faces as blank as Noh masks. It was obvious they had already been talking about this behind my back.

I fumbled desperately for an excuse.

'I—I'm sorry. I'm sure Mizuho didn't mean anything by it. She was just having fun.'

Akemi-san let out a cold laugh.

'Generally, the one getting laughed at isn't having fun.'

Ohh, I've just made her angrier. I need to apologize.

'I'm really sorry if Anri-chan felt upset. I'll make sure to have a talk with Mizuho about it.'

Crossing her arms, Akemi-san looked away. 'I wouldn't expect a high-society person living in a fancy new condo to understand.'

So *this* is what she thought of me.

'I'm not high-society,' I said quietly.

'Sure you are. We certainly can't afford to live

in Advance Hill on my husband's salary. You were such a star worker that you were even featured in the media, so you probably have a different perspective about these things.'

'That's not—'

'It's like what you said on our group LINE chat. When we all complimented you about the article, you said it was nothing. To you, I suppose it was nothing. That must be nice. You know, you've always been a bit passive in our conversations, like you're only half listening.'

My mind went completely blank.

I wanted to get up and leave that very second.

But if I ran away now, it might have consequences for Mizuho later. There was no telling what Akemi-san might tell Anri-chan—that she couldn't play with Mizuho any more, or worse, that Mizuho was a bully.

I had to protect Mizuho. I had to tamp down my emotions somehow and make things right.

But what exactly did it really mean to protect her?

Shouldn't I be clearing her name of these baseless accusations?

What should I say? How should I say it? I couldn't find the words.

I remained speechless, while Akemi-san leaned back in her chair and let out a heavy sigh.

'Oh, never mind. I wasn't blaming anyone. I just thought you should know, that's all. I hope Anri and Mizuho-chan can keep on being friends.'

'I'm sorry . . .'

'I said it's all right. Just forget it.'

Looking down, I mumbled a soft 'Thank you', stinging with dissatisfaction.

~

After, I was effectively frozen out of the group.

Even when I was nearby, the three mum friends would continue talking as if I wasn't there and did the Samantha without me.

Then suddenly, Akemi-san would act overly friendly and ask me for small favours, making it impossible to know how to maintain any distance.

The one saving grace was that Mizuho and Anri-chan continued to get along without any issues. But I couldn't be sure about what might happen next.

One time, when I was standing by myself at the stop, I noticed Kinugawa-san was also alone. Even so, I couldn't find an excuse to strike up a conversation. She always seemed focused solely on seeing off her son Tomoki-kun at the bus stop and waiting for his return.

How easy would things be if I could be like that, I thought. But Kinugawa-san and I were different. She had maintained this stance from the very beginning, whereas I had joined the mum group after it had already been established. I had to repair the relationship somehow; otherwise, things would continue to be tense right up until Mizuho graduated from kindergarten. These were pretend friendships, they were not real, and I wanted to manage the situation for Mizuho's sake.

The weekend when there was no kindergarten was truly a relief.

On a rare Sunday when Yoshitaka was not working, I decided to leave Mizuho with him and go to Asahi Store alone.

Realizing that I wouldn't have to hold Mizuho's hand, I decided to stop by the cleaners. I gathered several of Yoshitaka's shirts from his closet, a white blouse that needed de-staining, and a smock that

Mizuho had spilled paint on. I stuffed them into a paper bag and left the house.

The autumn sky was clear and pleasant. Walking alone, feeling the wind on my skin, was more than enough to bring me relief.

Although I washed most of our clothes in the washing machine, when the need arose I went to Sunrise Cleaning. An elderly woman with short hair was always at the counter. Although it took a bit longer for the cleaning to be ready, the price was reasonable, and the clothes came back spotless.

The elderly woman was alone at the store as usual, and when she saw me come in, she greeted me with a smile. 'Oh, Himura-san.' She remembered my name, even though I didn't visit all that often.

After she counted the number of shirts and checked the stains on the blouse and the smock, she commented, 'It's gotten a lot more comfortable lately, hasn't it? The summer was a scorcher this year.'

'Yes, the wind feels nice today.'

As I took the ticket from her, the door opened behind me.

When I saw who it was, I let out a small gasp.

It was Shizukuda-san.

She wasn't wearing her usual dark green polo shirt or her badge, but I recognized her right away in her yellow top.

She also seemed to recognize me, her face brightening into a smile.

'Hello.'

Her voice rang in my ears. She was just as friendly as she had been when I first saw her outside the supermarket.

I said hello back and stepped away from the counter to give her space.

She appeared to be picking up her cleaning. She handed the elderly woman a claim ticket and unfolded a large nylon bag.

The woman disappeared into the back and returned with the cleaning.

'One of the buttons on Mifuyu-chan's jacket was coming loose, so I sewed it back on for you.'

'Oh, I didn't notice. Thank you.'

Inside the plastic was a navy school uniform. Ah, so she had a daughter in school.

As I stood there, oddly riveted, Shizukuda-san turned to me with a cheerful smile. 'The service here is wonderful, isn't it? They even do repairs on clothes at reasonable prices. And she's also a pro at sewing kimonos.'

'If you take care of your clothes, you can wear them for a very long time,' said the elderly woman proudly.

'You're the Kabahiko of Sunrise Cleaning!'

Shizukuda-san and the elderly woman exchanged a look and laughed.

'Kabahiko?'

It was the first time I'd heard the name. Noticing my puzzled expression, Shizukuda-san explained, 'It's the name of the hippo at Hinode Park just up the way.'

'Yes, I know it!'

It was the orange animal ride at the park. So his name was Kabahiko.

'Legend has it that if you touch the hippo on the part of your body that needs healing, Kabahiko will make it better.'

'*What?*' I exclaimed in earnest surprise.

With a serious look, the elderly woman added, 'It's true. I rubbed Kabahiko's back, and he cured my herniated disk.'

Who knew that paint-chipped hippo had that kind of power?

'That's why they call him Healing Kabahiko,' proclaimed Shizukuda-san.

'Get it?' the elderly woman said softly. 'Because Kaba-*hiko* sounds like *hippo*.'

I felt my cheeks slacken.

'Although, I suspect few people truly believe that. That poor hippo isn't much to look at,' she carried on, her face sagging into a comically sad expression.

I gave them both a smile, but inwardly, my heart was racing.

Urban legend or not, who would have thought that I would find what I was looking for so close at hand—a salve for something no medicine could cure, something I desperately wanted to heal.

I bowed politely to excuse myself and left the store.

My feet carried me straight to the park. The playground was empty, though Kabahiko was there as usual, as though he'd been waiting for me. His carefree face and stumpy body suddenly seemed adorable to me.

'Kabahiko,' I murmured aloud.

I reached out and placed my palm on his mouth, which stretched right across his face.

Please, Kabahiko.

Turn me back into the person I was when I could speak freely.

Repair my relationship with the mum group. Please. I'm begging you.

Kabahiko stood there, smiling. I rubbed his mouth over and over with my hand as my eyes misted with tears.

~

The following week, the bazaar committee held a meeting.

We gathered upstairs at the kindergarten an hour before school let out so we could pick up our children right after the meeting.

Akemi-san and her mum group seemed to have come together and were sitting in a tight group. Around ten more mums had also turned up, and were clustered about the room in conversation. I sat in a seat in the corner, idly flipping through my planner.

Akemi-san presided over the meeting, quickly taking charge. From collecting donations to sorting and pricing, she assigned roles and created a schedule with remarkable efficiency. Each mum was put in charge of a section: household goods, foods, handicrafts or games. Decisions were made quickly, due entirely to Akemi-san's assertive style, and every time the meeting stalled, she had people draw straws to decide, leaving no room for objection.

One mother raised a concern about what would happen to the unsold items. Having served on the bazaar committee when her oldest was at another kindergarten, she remembered feeling guilty about throwing away unsold goods and how trying to sell them the next year often didn't work out.

Akemi-san answered nonchalantly, 'Why don't we have each of the sellers take responsibility for their section? If anything remains unsold, they can just buy it themselves.'

Akemi-san was in charge of games, a section that always sold out.

There were murmurs, but no one voiced any

objection. She then insisted, 'Everyone should do their best to sell out their section. And if that doesn't work, you can put the leftover items on Mercari. If you can get a good price for them, you'll make out with some extra spending money.'

She acted as though she'd come up with a brilliant idea.

Glancing at the wall clock, she announced, 'Well, it's about time to wrap up the meeting.' Just then—

'I'm not sure.'

A voice rose from across the room, and instantly, the gathering fell silent. I looked over, and caught a flash of long, black hair.

It was Kinugawa-san. In a calm, clarion tone, she continued, 'We were all assigned equal roles. Of course, we should do our best to sell what we can, but I don't think it should be anyone's responsibility to pay out-of-pocket for unsold items.'

'Well . . . then . . .' Caught off guard, Akemi-san faltered. 'What do you suggest we do about it, Kinugawa-san?'

'I'd like for us to come up with a solution together. Does that sound all right?'

Kinugawa-san wore a gentle smile.

Her smile seemed strangely familiar. I gasped.

Kabahiko?

What was I thinking? Mistaking Kinugawa-san for Kabahiko at a time like this.

The slender and cool-tempered Kinugawa-san and the roly-poly hippo with the silly smile were nothing alike.

Somewhere deep inside me, a mass of ice started to thaw.

'Um . . .'

My voice slipped out before I realized it.

Akemi-san's eyes widened as she looked this way. But it was too late—the words were already slipping out.

'Maybe we could set some conditions when we first collect the donated items. We could say, for example, that we won't accept any unappealing prize items or freebies.'

I recalled a similar suggestion from a mother on the bazaar committee at the previous school. The mother who had raised the concern earlier nodded in agreement.

'Yes, that's a good idea. Those little toys that come with kids' meals don't sell at all.'

Others, who had been silent until then, began to offer suggestions.

'Someone should check the condition of the clothes and shoes before accepting them. People tend to bring items that are too old or damaged.'

'In the afternoon, we can bundle items and sell them at a lower cost.'

'What if we give away the unsold accessories and toys as prizes in the games corner?'

Akemi-san's mouth was in a deep pout, but when Kinugawa-san asked deferentially, 'We'd appreciate it if you'd organize us, Nishimoto-san,' her mood seemed to warm.

Akemi-san took the lead in collecting everyone's opinions, then took a look around the room. 'Let's all work together to make this a fun bazaar.'

With that, the meeting ended, and the mothers filed out.

～

My chest was racing.

Just as Kinugawa-san was about to leave, I gathered the courage to call out to her. She turned around, and before I knew it, the words were tumbling out of my mouth.

'Thank you, *thank you*.'

It was the first time in a while that I felt genuine gratitude. She gave me a puzzled smile.

I desperately tried to find the right words.

'Thanks to you, I was able to speak up.'

It was only then that I fully understood.

Kinugawa-san greeted us every day at the bus stop with a 'Good morning', but none of the mothers, including myself, ever responded.

But Kinugawa-san wasn't silent. She spoke more than anyone else when it came to important matters. It was only during the meeting that I realized her quiet strength.

I wanted to be someone who could speak with confidence again.

But it wasn't just about talking more.

It was about being able to say what needed to be said.

'I felt supported when you were the first to speak up.'

Kinugawa-san broke into a wide smile. In that moment, she reminded me of Kabahiko—

Steady, composed and always with a warm grin.

'Didn't you have work today?' I asked, a little more boldly this time.

Kinugawa-san shook her head. 'Today's my day off.'

I gathered my courage. 'What kind of work do you do?'

'I run a yoga studio in a separate annexe at my house.'

A yoga studio!

It suited her so perfectly that everything made sense—her upright posture, steady mindset and slightly mysterious aura.

'I considered putting Tomoki in daycare when he was a bit younger, but since I work part-time from home, I had a difficult time getting approved,' she said. 'Then, as soon as we got into the kindergarten, my husband got transferred and had to live away for work.'

She chuckled and shrugged. If I'd known she would open up like this, I would have reached out to her sooner. Maybe I was the one who had built a wall and kept my distance from her.

'Then you're completely on your own at home?' I asked, no longer using formal language.

She nodded emphatically.

'That's why if I don't set my own pace, nothing gets done. The school officers have duties throughout the school year. The bazaar committee, on the other hand, can be a lot of work, but it's short-term and focused, so I can adjust my schedule around it, so that's why I joined.'

Oh. I couldn't help but sigh. She was nothing like me. I had been pushed into joining the bazaar committee by Akemi-san.

Kinugawa-san and I went downstairs to the classroom on the first floor, where our kids were waiting. The usual trio of mums, led by Akemi-san, and their kids were already gone.

In the corner of the room, Tomoki-kun and Mizuho were sitting together, folding origami. That's right. Regardless of what was going on with the parents, kids managed to find playmates on their own. Mizuho noticed our arrival and pattered towards me.

'Mummy! Tomoki-kun showed me how to make this.'

In her tiny hand was a pink origami flower.

Something was written inside the white circle in the centre in Mizuho's innocent handwriting.

Sawa Himura

My name.
'It's for you, Mummy.'
Mizuho tilted her head and beamed. A rolled piece of tape was stuck to the back of the flower.
A brand-new name badge from my daughter.

~

November, the day of the bazaar.
I stood in the clothing section, arranging and tagging items—mostly children's clothes.
When someone approached looking keen to buy, I felt a rush of joy course through me. It was a feeling I hadn't experienced in years. Though the size of the store and the products I was now selling were completely different, I was practically dancing with excitement. I realized just how much I loved interacting with customers.

I knew I wanted to find a job. I could start part-time, doing whatever I was capable of for now. Something bright bubbled up from inside me, not exactly confidence but a simple desire to challenge myself.

Since that day, I no longer felt anxious about going to the bus stop for drop-offs and pick-ups.

I greeted everyone with a cheerful 'Good morning', chatted when necessary and waved at Mizuho, smiling as she beamed from the bus. That was plenty. That was what this time was for.

Instead of doing the Samantha with the others, I occasionally went to Kinugawa-san's yoga studio.

Yes, I had repaired my relationship with the mum group. I could be myself now, without pretence, and in a way that suited me. I wouldn't let myself be swept up by the others anymore. I would do what needed to be done and what I wanted to do, carefully, at my own pace.

Pinned to my chest was a lovely flower-shaped name badge.

This world wasn't a 'pretend' one. I was living in this reality as Mizuho's one and only mother, as Sawa Himura.

A woman stopped in front of the display and picked up a blouse.

I struck up a conversation, pointing out the texture of the blouse, the quality of the stitching, and what bottoms would pair well with it.

The customer's eyes softened into a smile. 'Okay, I'll take it.'

She handed me the payment and walked away. '*Thank you*,' I said, my heart brimming with gratitude.

3

Chiharu's Ears

'Chiharu Niizawa.'

I stood up from my chair when my name was called.

The waiting room of the ENT clinic, which I was visiting for the first time, was surprisingly crowded.

'Yes?'

My voice reverberated uncomfortably in my ears. The echo was unsettling.

How did it come to this?

For some time now, I'd been plagued by a sensation of fullness in my ears.

It wasn't pain, nor was it that I couldn't hear

outside sounds, rather an indescribable discomfort that engulfed me.

It wasn't just my voice. Even the sound of my breathing echoed in my ears and head. Being constantly aware of it throughout the day was unbearable.

Growing up, I had always been healthy and rarely had to go to hospital. I didn't even know which ENT clinics were any good, let alone know how to go about finding one.

A nurse led me into the examination room, where a shy-looking, elderly doctor was sitting. He calmly asked me questions and wrote down my answers on a medical chart.

Using a silver instrument with a funnel-shaped tip to examine my ears, the doctor asked, 'Have you been eating?'

'Not much,' I replied, and my voice seemed to bounce back inside my ears.

The doctor nodded. 'You must have lost weight recently.'

His eyes seemed filled with pity. For a moment, I wanted to cry.

It was as if he had said, *You must be unhappy.*

~

When I woke up, it was already past noon.

I sat on the couch in the living room, picked up the remote and turned on the TV.

Talk shows, repeats of old dramas, the shopping channel—all so boring. There was nothing I wanted to watch. Then I thought: *Get over yourself. You're not in any position to complain, even at the TV.* Basically, I had had enough of my lazy self, sprawling on the couch in my pajamas on a weekday afternoon.

Patulous Eustachian tube dysfunction.

That was the name of the condition I was diagnosed with.

'It's when the Eustachian tube, which is normally closed, stays open,' explained the doctor. 'I can't say for certain what's causing this, but it might be due to sudden weight loss, a lack of sleep or . . .'

He paused to take a breath, then continued as if wrapping things up.

'It's usually triggered by stress or overwork. I can prescribe medication, but you might do better by resting first. If you need a medical certificate, I can provide one for you.'

At that moment, the condition, likely caused by stress, was itself the source of stress for me.

I worked at a bridal production company. My duties included customer service, sales calls and overseeing various arrangements. The job of a wedding planner involved a wide range of tasks, both big and small.

A wedding was a joyous once-in-a-lifetime event for clients, so it was essential to maintain a smile at all times. Yet, with my voice seeming to bounce back at me every time I spoke, even greeting someone was exhausting. In time, this only added to my stress, creating a negative loop that I couldn't escape.

For this reason, I requested both the medical certificate and the medication. I was desperate.

The doctor prescribed me some Chinese herbal medicine. It wasn't meant to heal the ear issue directly, but to improve my mental well-being and blood circulation.

I remembered the doctor's pitying words suggesting that I must have suddenly lost weight.

I had actually lost over five kilograms in a month. I was always on the slim side, and people around me were usually astonished by how much I ate despite my size. But recently, I had no appetite at all and could only manage to force down some jelly cups to get by.

My weight, which had been in the mid-forty-kilogram range on my 160cm frame, was dropping rapidly. Once it reached the thirty-kilogram range, I became too afraid to step on the scale.

I turned off the TV, got up and headed into the kitchen.

I had to eat something.

But first, I opened a sachet of herbal medicine, which I was supposed to take before meals. The Chinese characters on the silver packet made my illness feel even more real.

Two weeks had passed since I'd taken a leave of absence from work.

But I had no confidence that I was spending my leave restfully. When the company approved my leave, I had felt relieved, yet the more time passed, the more I questioned whether I was doing the right thing.

Both my parents were teachers, leaving the house early in the morning and not returning until late at night. My father worked at a private high school, my mother at a public junior high school. As the youngest of the household, I felt guilty being the one lounging around at home.

Though I was undergoing treatment, I didn't require surgery or hospitalization. I was simply waiting for my ears to return to normal while resting my body and trying to eat a little more each day.

Since there was no fever or pain, I knew it would be difficult for people to understand my misery. It wasn't something you could see, and it felt as though I had entered a dark tunnel with no exit, frustrated by the uncertainty of what lay ahead.

The feeling of congestion in my ears eased when I lay down. The muffled sensation would subside and return to normal. So, whenever the symptoms became overwhelming, I would collapse onto the couch.

I often tried to at least read a book, but lying down caused me to doze off with the paperback still in my hands. Then I wouldn't be able to sleep that night or wake up in the morning, creating a vicious cycle.

It wasn't just my ears; I could also feel myself growing more and more closed off.

Even if my ears improved, I worried whether I

would be able to return to work with the same energy I once had. Thinking about it depressed me.

I graduated from university, joined the company and by the time I was twenty-six, I had been working for three years.

I started out assisting my senior colleagues, and eventually I was entrusted with managing clients on my own, which should have felt fulfilling.

I had always dreamed of working in the bridal industry.

Becoming a wedding planner and witnessing people's happiness brought me true joy.

I used to love my job.

But then I thought of Sumie, a colleague in my department, and a bitterness rose from the pit of my stomach.

Her large eyes, accentuated by eyelash extensions, her crystalline, high-pitched voice—her natural cheerfulness riled me.

She had transferred from another bridal company six months ago. Although she was a year younger than me, she had started working right after graduating from a specialty school, so she had more experience.

Where Sumie spoke and made decisions quickly, I preferred to take my time, getting to know my clients more thoroughly. Our supervisor had once told me it wasn't a matter of one approach being better than the other. Still, Sumie's significantly higher closing rate was undeniable.

It might be an exaggeration to say I became ill because of her, but it was true her presence left me with no breathing room.

Unable to make my sales target, I was overcome with unrelenting anxiety. Small mistakes began piling up; each time I made one, I was really hard on myself. I overreacted to every client's response, which only wore down my confidence.

I wondered whether I needed to become more like Sumie.

I was just so tired. Tired of everything.

I poured myself a glass of water and washed the granulated herbal medicine down my throat. It had a strange taste that I couldn't quite describe. I could hardly believe that this would actually make me better.

With the afternoon sun streaming in, the living room was full of light.

Unable to decide what to eat, I opened the window and looked outside.

We had moved to this condominium in April. It was a newly built five-storey building called Advance Hill, the place my parents referred to as their final residence.

They were honest people. They had worked hard—without ever once straying from their straight path—and had saved all their money to purchase the condominium.

Having worked in classrooms for many years, they didn't pry about my condition. They might have come across students who had been incapacitated by various circumstances before.

From the third-storey balcony of our home, I had an unobstructed view of the sky without the building across the way blocking anything.

It was a crisp autumn day in October. The perfect day for a wedding. And what was I doing during this busy wedding season?

On days like this, it felt as though everyone around the world was celebrating the beauty of the outdoors. But here I was, shut away. The cloudless sky only deepened my misery, and that pained me.

~

'Oh, drat. We're out of eggs,' my mother said, standing in front of the refrigerator after dinner.

Eggs were essential for my mother to make bentos every morning.

It was past 9 p.m. The nearest supermarket was already closed.

I got up from the couch.

'I'll go buy some at the convenience store. You need them for tomorrow morning, don't you?'

'It's okay, we can do without eggs for lunch.' My mother closed the refrigerator door and gave me a smile.

I pulled on a hooded jacket and slipped my smartphone in the pocket. 'I'm going out for a walk. I could use the exercise.'

That was true.

I knew it would do me good to move around a bit, but during the day I couldn't shake off my sluggishness. I always felt a bit more energetic after the sun went down.

'Be careful.'

'Okay.'

At this hour, most people had already finished work and were relaxing at home.

This made me feel a little better.

I didn't need to feel so guilty because I wasn't working. Helping out around the house also helped calm me down, even if it was just going to the convenience store to buy eggs.

I slung a tote bag with my wallet over my shoulder and went outside.

I strolled steadily along the sidewalk, staring down at my sneakers. When I looked up, car headlights and traffic lights winked in the darkness.

At that moment, the LINE notification pinged.

I took out my smartphone from my jacket pocket.

The screen lit up with a string of texts.

How are you feeling?

It was from Yoji Shimatani, a colleague from work.

My heart began to race.

I had intended to just look at the notification and not open the app, but I accidentally touched the screen, marking it as read.

I had no choice. I stopped at the side of the street and typed a brief reply:

Same, I guess.

Almost immediately, my message was marked as read, and a speech bubble appeared:

Oh. Same on my end. Had three temporary reservations cancelled in a row.

A sticker of a crying rabbit appeared.

I stared in a daze at the rabbit.

Even during my leave of absence, Yoji occasionally contacted me like this.

What did he want from me? What was I supposed to do?

Yoji was polite and personable, so it was difficult to read his true feelings. This made me feel as if I were being deceived. He didn't realize that his kind smile was hurting someone.

In that sense, he and Sumie were alike.

There had been numerous times I had felt secretly hurt by him. Even so, I'd never once told him about it. Since we had to see each other at work, I didn't want things to get awkward.

All I had to do was grin and bear it. That was all.

When I was feeling well I might have been able to smile and play it cool, but in my current condition Yoji was someone I'd rather not see. In fact, he was someone I was afraid to see—second only to Sumie.

All I could do was keep my distance and try not to think about what his true intentions were.

I put my phone back in my pocket without sending a reply.

I started walking again, and as I got to the convenience store, the LINE notification pinged again.

It was probably from Yoji. I didn't want to look.

I browsed aimlessly around the store, bought the eggs and, after placing them carefully in my tote bag, I finally checked my phone.

Let's both take it easy. Don't push yourself too hard.

How sweet of him.

I couldn't bring myself to smile as I gripped my phone.

I sent him a sticker of a cat bowing its head in thanks and closed the screen.

~

After ending my LINE conversation with Yoji, I felt restless and couldn't bring myself to go straight home.

Instead of going back the way I came, I wandered into a residential neighbourhood and spotted an old house with a dry cleaners on the ground floor. The store with the red overhang bearing the words 'Sunrise Cleaning' was closed.

It had probably been there for years, serving the local residents.

On a whim, I bought a can of hot coffee from the vending machine outside the store.

I didn't feel particularly chilly, but the warmth of the can felt good on my hands. That was when I realized my fingers were cold.

Rather than putting the coffee can in my bag, I kept it in my hands while I walked. The narrow promenade wound gently through an apartment complex.

The light from people's rooms filtered through curtains, scattering colours in uneven hues. Some of them seemed to have their windows open, and a mix of sound and smells drifted through the air.

Inside those square boxes were so many apartments, each with a family living there.

Many people must have got married.

And many more would, no doubt, in the future.

I wondered if I would get married someday.

As my thoughts wandered with no clear destination, a park came into view. A grey rock slab at the entrance had the words 'Hinode Park' engraved on it.

Hinode.

Sunrise.

Oh, so the name of the cleaners must have come from the name of the town.

The park was empty. There were two streetlamps flanking the entrance and two more at the back. Beneath the glow of the fluorescent lights, something short and squat glowed.

It was a stationary hippo ride.

Feeling relieved at the sight of this comforting, innocuous figure, I moved towards it.

113

The paint was peeling off in places, its black eyes turned partly white, making it look as though it was tearing up. Yet, its mouth was curled into an endearing smile.

The sight of the hippo, looking innocently up at me, melted my heart.

I sat side-saddle on it and placed my hand on its rounded back.

I pulled the tab on the coffee can. When I brought it to my lips, a pleasant aroma filled my nostrils. I took a small sip, the sound echoing deep inside my ears. *Sip.*

I still hadn't gotten used to it. When would my condition get better?

When I was diagnosed with Patulous Eustachian tube dysfunction, the kanji characters didn't immediately come to mind.

When I heard the name, I thought of its Japanese homonym, which was 'time release'.

Perhaps it was a manifestation of my desire to turn back time, back to more enjoyable days.

Taking advantage of the fact I was wearing jeans, I threw one leg over the hippo's back.

Suddenly, I remembered a client named Inashiro-san.

'Could I maybe make an entrance on a white horse?' the fifty-five-year-old man had exclaimed.

He was so enormous, he was almost three times the size of his bride. He always leaned forward, talking excitedly.

Other times, he'd ask, 'Could someone get us a video of a congratulatory message from a celebrity?' or 'I'd like Yuna to change out of her wedding dress into a traditional white kimono, and we want at least five wardrobe changes,' and made numerous other astronomical demands on a tight budget.

It was Inashiro-san's first marriage and his bride, Yuna-san, was fifteen years younger. Beautiful with well-proportioned features, she looked like she could be a model. She hardly spoke but sat quietly next to Inashiro-san.

The bride was usually in charge of what she wanted for the wedding. It was rare to get such passionate requests from the groom.

Despite slightly resenting this difficult client, I was also inwardly touched. He was, after all, so very earnest. Since I ended up as their planner, I took pleasure in trying to make Inashiro-san's wishes come true, even if just a little.

However, the condition of my ears gradually worsened, and Inashiro-san was my last client before I took leave.

Though I tried my best to hide my illness, I couldn't be sure that our communication was as smooth as it should have been during that crucial time leading up to the wedding.

On the day of the ceremony, Inashiro-san had seemed thoroughly displeased, and we only exchanged a few words before parting.

It had been on my mind ever since. As anxious as I was, I hadn't been able to ask Inashiro-san if I had fallen short in some way.

Anxious. Yes, I was always anxious.

About what others thought of me. About whether I was doing my job properly.

What was I going to do now? What was going to happen to me? My anxiety only grew.

Still sitting on the hippo, I sipped my coffee.

Just me and the hippo in the park at night. The

air felt still and cool, calming the unease that had unsettled my heart.

I bent forward at the waist, resting my cheek on the hippo's head.

I'll come here again. For now, this guy is the only companion I need.

~

'Ah, I forgot to send this out to the cleaners.'

After my mother's eggs, it was my father's turn.

Last night, seemingly remembering something just before bed, my father had started rummaging through the closet.

The following week, his high school was holding a ceremony to mark its fiftieth anniversary. My father held up a navy suit and scowled.

As a P.E. teacher, he hardly ever wore a proper suit. As far as I knew, he only owned the one.

After wearing the suit to this year's entrance ceremony, he had shoved it back in the overstuffed closet and forgotten about it.

The collar was misshapen and creased, the hem

frayed and worn. The suit needed to be cleaned, of course, but more than that, it looked like it needed a good pressing.

'Would you like me to drop it off at the cleaners tomorrow?'

My father's face brightened at my offer. 'Would you?'

'Sure, I happened to find a cleaner recently.'

I wanted to use this as a reason to get up and go in the morning. I needed to correct my upside-down schedule anyway.

Despite my offer, I still ended up dragging my feet when I woke up and didn't leave the house until sometime past three.

I slid open the door to Sunrise Cleaning and found a small elderly woman sitting behind the counter. She lifted her head and looked at me.

'Welcome.'

I laid my father's suit on the counter. The elderly woman put on her glasses and looked over the suit carefully.

'Someone's been wearing this for a while. Is it your father's?'

She chuckled. Suits had trends, too. She might be scoffing at how outdated the style of the suit was.

'Yes,' I answered, 'I'm embarrassed to say.'

I shrugged, and the woman gave me a serious look.

'Don't be! Maintaining an item of clothing and wearing it for a long time is a wonderful thing. It's the same as maintaining the body.'

'*The body?*'

Perhaps my voice was too soft to be heard. The elderly woman didn't answer but instead traced her fingertip along the edge of the suit's lapel.

'But it seems your father isn't very good at maintaining it. Leave it to me. I'll have it looking like new again.'

She skillfully tore off a claim ticket.

I paid the fee, took the claim ticket from her, and left the store, my steps leading me towards Hinode Park. Toward the hippo.

There was already someone there. A familiar face.

It was Himura-san, who lived on the second floor of the condominiums. Her daughter, Mizuho-chan, was with her.

The Himura residence was located just below our unit, so when they first moved in, my parents and I went as a family to welcome them with a gift of towels.

It seemed Mizuho-chan was in kindergarten. Come to think of it, we also met at the model room viewing. I remembered thinking how adorable the little girl was.

Himura-san was probably in her mid-thirties. She was always so well put together.

It wasn't that she wore expensive clothes, but rather that her clean, casual style was lovely. I thought she was stylish for being able to wear everyday clothes with such good taste.

Mizuho-chan was happily pumping her legs on the swings.

Himura-san was sitting on the hippo's back.

I was considering coming back another time when Himura-san noticed me.

'Oh, hi, Chiharu-chan.' She smiled amiably.

Thinking it would be rude to leave now, I carried on into the park.

Despite my wandering around in a baggy sweat-shirt and denim skirt at this hour, she didn't try to ask about my work. I was relieved that she accepted me as I was.

Since I often had weekdays off when I was working, perhaps I was just being overly self-conscious to think that way.

Himura-san had her shoulder bag strapped diagonally across her body and held a tote bag with a keyboard design in her hand. The latter probably belonged to Mizuho-chan.

'This park is wonderful, isn't it? It's a bit tucked away, so it doesn't get much sun, but maybe that's why not many people come here. I come here sometimes, too, to see him.'

Oh, Himura-san too?

'Do you know about Kabahiko's legend?' she asked brightly.

'Is this guy named Kabahiko?'

'So,' she replied, 'they say that if you touch the same part on the hippo as the part of your body that needs healing, you feel better. They call him Healing Kabahiko. Get it? Because Kaba-*hiko* sounds like *hippo*.'

She held up a finger and gave me a playful smile.

'Do you have somewhere that needs . . .' I asked

a bit vaguely. Himura-san looked off in the distance. 'Yup, Kabahiko healed the part I wanted to make better. But if I get complacent again, it might come back. So, I visit the park occasionally to give him a rub.'

Like a maintenance check-in.

Recalling what the woman at the cleaners had said, I observed Himura-san's contented expression.

She rested her palm on Kabahiko's mouth and patted it as though comforting a child. After glancing at her watch, she turned around towards the swings.

'Mizuho, time to go to your piano lesson.'

'Okay!' the girl answered, and jumped off the swing.

'See you, Mizuho-chan,' I said.

The girl gave me a wave, and I waved back before bowing to Himura-san.

As soon as mother and daughter left the park, I crouched down in front of Kabahiko.

Healing Kabahiko.

What a charming name you have!

I reached for his ear and stroked it softly, ever so softly.

I didn't know why, but as I did so, I felt as though

Kabahiko himself was suffering from the same ear condition as I was.

It's tough, isn't it? So exhausting. You poor thing.

As I stroked Kabahiko's ear again and again, a bitter ache welled up from inside my chest. Memories of my difficulties at work came flooding back, one after another.

Demanding sales targets, complicated and tedious incidents, misunderstandings with external staff, complaints from clients—amidst it all, what lingered most vividly in my mind was those two colleagues.

Sumie. If only she wasn't around.

Yoji. It was all his fault.

It's your fault I've ended up like this.

You're probably laughing at me. Pretending to worry about me.

Why is it always me? Why am I the one who's always miserable?

Oh, but that LINE message from Yoji. He said he had three temporary reservations cancelled in a row.

He said it casually but that must have been quite a blow.

'Serves him right.'

The words slipped out of my mouth and echoed in my head, taking me aback.

Was that really my voice? It was as if the devil had whispered the words into my ear, making me shudder.

I was sneering just now. How hideous my face must look.

No, no, no, how could I?

I got up and ran out of the park.

~

The discomfort in my ears came and went, and I became more distressed.

Every time I felt myself getting better, the pain would return a few hours later. Just when I thought my appetite had returned, it would vanish the next morning. The fact that I wasn't able to control it left me utterly miserable.

When it rained for several days, the change in air pressure only made my condition worse.

Despite hearing the story of Kabahiko, I had kept my distance from the park.

Talking to Kabahiko had felt like putting my heart up to a mirror, and it terrified me.

I had completely forgotten about the dry cleaning. It wasn't until my father asked about his suit that I remembered.

I checked the claim ticket. It had been ready two days ago.

By evening, the rain had let up, so I grabbed a large paper bag to put the suit in and went out.

I opened the sliding door to Sunrise Cleaning.

The elderly woman who had been reading looked up and closed the magazine.

Before I could give her the claim ticket, she went into the back and returned to the counter with the navy suit wrapped in plastic.

Even through the clear plastic, I could tell the suit had been pressed crisply back to life.

Folding the resurrected suit carefully to avoid any wrinkles, I placed it into the paper bag. Then, the elderly woman extended her hand towards me.

'Here.'

Sitting on her hand was a candy wrapped in yellow cellophane.

I glanced at the counter and noticed an empty jelly jar sitting next to a pen stand, filled to the brim with the same candies.

I took the one from her hand, which had a picture of a bee on the wrapper. *Honey-flavoured.*

'It's good for you,' she said. 'You look a little pale.'

Her words brought tears to my eyes. Before I knew it, I was venting my frustrations.

'It's just . . . I feel so anxious about everything.'

Ev-ery . . . thing . . . My voice echoed over the self-pity welling up inside me.

'I think anxiety is evidence of a powerful imagination,' said the woman.

'*Imagination?*'

'That's right. Anxiety is something you feel about something that hasn't happened yet or about others. The fact that you can picture those things shows you have a good imagination.'

I feel anxious because of my imagination?

I'd never thought of it that way. I felt somewhat relieved and let out a deep sigh. 'I always thought that imagination was for positive things.'

'Sure, kindness and consideration are all part of imagination. I think someone as anxious as you must be a kind person.'

No . . . that's not true. I'm exhausted and struggle

with the ugly side of myself that blames others for things not going my way.

I held back the words and bit my lip.

The woman tilted her head.

'Instead of dwelling on the future or on someone else, try focusing on what you're feeling now. While enjoying a piece of candy or something.'

~

When I left the cleaners, it was past dusk, and the sun had set.

It was chillier than the last time I'd come. I could feel the season changing.

I walked towards the park, sucking on the honey-flavoured candy.

Hinode Park was as empty as usual, which brought me a sense of relief.

It felt like my very own hideout. It was as if Kabahiko was waiting for me.

I approached the hippo and set the paper bag down at my feet.

When I crouched in front of him, his eyes were perfectly level with mine.

I looked at his relaxed face, slowly rolling the candy around in my mouth.

It might have been just my imagination, but sucking on the candy seemed to ease the discomfort in my ears, its simple, nostalgic sweetness melting on my tongue.

Instead of dwelling on the future or someone else, try focusing on what you're feeling now.

There before me was Kabahiko's roly-poly head.

I placed my hands on his cheeks, then moved them up to his forehead before gently resting them on his ears, stroking them slowly.

'*I loved him*,' I whispered out loud.

Kabahiko was listening. Or at least, that was how it seemed.

I confessed what was in my heart, pouring out all my feelings.

~

I had been in love with Yoji from the very beginning. I thought I was closer to him than anyone else.

We were the only two who started at the company that year.

We hit it off right away, talking about all sorts of things.

We motivated each other to work hard towards becoming great wedding planners. When we were both free, we'd go out together to research new restaurants, collect and study wedding venue pamphlets across Japan, and push each other to hit our sales targets, betting on an all-you-can-eat yakiniku meal as a reward.

He'd told me he enjoyed spending time with me, that he could talk to me about anything.

Interpreting his words as signs of affection, I completely let myself believe that, in time, I could become his girlfriend.

I was always by his side, watching his face.

Because of that, I was the first to notice Yoji and Sumie were drawn to each other.

But I couldn't bring myself to confront it directly. I was afraid to admit it.

One day, on my way back from a business call, I saw them outside a French restaurant on a date.

They didn't notice me standing there, frozen. They were gazing into each other's eyes and laughing.

If they were having an innocent meal together

simply because their lunch breaks lined up, it might not have meant anything.

Just because Yoji, who was open with everyone, and outgoing Sumie were researching restaurants together didn't mean they were involved.

But when I saw Yoji's hand on the small of her back as they stood outside our building entrance, I knew.

That wasn't a gesture meant for a friend.

I had not heard any rumours at work.

Either they were good at keeping their relationship private or maybe it was my misunderstanding, and they were nothing more than good colleagues. I couldn't be sure.

That was when my ears, which were already causing me discomfort, began to get worse.

A few days later, Yoji said, 'I have some news. Are you free for a drink?'

He smiled shyly, and I knew it had to be about Sumie.

I made up an excuse and turned him down.

Meanwhile, the discomfort in my ears worsened, and I ended up taking my leave of absence before I could talk to Yoji.

Why not me? I thought helplessly over and over again.

Why did you choose Sumie over me, Yoji?

After you led me on like you did.

Sumie, don't take Yoji and my job away from me.

Don't destroy everything I've worked so hard to build.

How dare you? How dare the both of you?

You two will never find happiness, not after how unhappy you've made me.

Kabahiko was looking at me with his dewy eyes as though he understood everything.

As I stared at his face, a huge sigh escaped me.

No, that's not it.

Deep down, I knew.

Neither Yoji nor Sumie was to blame.

All they did was work hard and fall in love.

And here I was, self-destructing all on my own.

Without the courage to confront the truth or express my feelings for Yoji, I had run away.

Because I was too afraid to face the truth about them. Because I didn't want to know.

I continued to stroke Kabahiko's ears.

Help me, Kabahiko.

My ears refused to accept the painful truth.

My ears, crushed by my anxious imagination, shut themselves off to everything but my own voice.

Every emotion I projected outwards came right back to me.

Help me, Kabahiko. Heal me, please. Restore me to the person I used to be. The person who could wish for the happiness of others.

~

The next morning, a letter arrived at my home.

It was from the office. I opened the envelope, fearing it might contain a suggestion that I resign. Inside, there was another envelope.

A sticky note from the administrative department read: *Please find enclosed a letter from a client.*

The sender was Inashiro-san.

I froze. What did he want with me? Was it a complaint?

For a moment, I could only stare at the envelope.

The characters were boldly written with a brush.

It was as if Inashiro-san, with his imposing frame and loud voice, had materialized on the envelope.

Taking a deep breath, I sat down at the dining table and carefully unfolded the letter.

To Chiharu Niizawa:

I hope this letter finds you well.

This is Inashiro, whose wedding ceremony you planned. I remain truly grateful for your assistance during that time.

I recently called your office about another matter and was surprised to hear you were unwell and taking some time off. How are you feeling?

Please excuse me for not properly thanking you after the ceremony. On the wedding day, I was so overwhelmed with emotions that not only was I barely able to sleep the night before but it was all I could do to keep from panicking in front of the guests.

Despite my size, I'm afraid I have the heart of a flea.

Thanks to you, the wedding was truly wonderful. My relatives and friends all said it was a lovely ceremony. But what I found most remarkable was our meetings leading up to the day.

I am writing to you because I wanted to share that with you.

As you know, this is my first marriage. I had always assumed I would remain single. I didn't think that would be so bad. But then, well into my fifties, I met Yuna and fell in love with her instantly.

I'm embarrassed to admit she is my first love.

I tried to win her heart the best way I could, but as you know, she is quite beautiful. People kept saying, 'Impossible, let it go. You can't possibly be with her.' Even after she somehow took an interest in me, they laughed and said, 'She's just playing with you. You can't possibly marry her.'

I had become accustomed to being told 'impossible' and 'you can't'—accustomed to people thinking that way no matter what I did.

I was even told outright that our marriage,

which I'd worked so hard to achieve, wouldn't last.

But, Niizawa-san, no matter how unreasonable my requests were, you never once said they were impossible.

You made the sincerest effort to find the best possible solution to fulfill my wishes, even for things that I thought couldn't be done.

All the requests I made had come from Yuna. She's quite soft-spoken, so I acted on her behalf. I was determined to make Yuna happy. This is her second marriage. The first time, she only registered the marriage without having a ceremony. I wanted to give her the wedding of her dreams.

With this in mind, as we consulted you about various things, I found myself enjoying planning the wedding with you. You understood how important this day was for both of us, and we felt your support in everything you did.

Thank you.

Yuna also expressed how fortunate we were

to have you as our wedding planner. Though I may be completely under Yuna's thumb, we get along very well. I'm hopeful that will continue. No matter who says it's impossible, whenever we think of you, we feel reassured that we will be all right.

Could it be that you were already unwell around the time of our wedding? I was so caught up in my own affairs that I didn't think to consider your well-being, and for that, I'm sorry.

Please take time to rest and recover at your own pace.

I'm certain future brides and grooms will be eagerly awaiting your return.

Saburo Inashiro

Oh, so that's it. That's what it was.
'Thank goodness,' I murmured.
Warm tears tumbled down my cheeks, and I began to sob softly.
I had believed Inashiro-san's hard expression on his wedding day meant that he was dissatisfied with me—that I had somehow lost his trust.

I was relieved to know that my intentions had reached him, and that the couple was happy.

I couldn't believe how foolishly I'd misunderstood things. My baseless assumptions led me down such unnecessary paths.

If only I had faced the situation head-on, I would have understood much sooner.

Inashiro-san.

Whoever told you that it was impossible was probably just envious, seeing how perfect you and Yuna-san are together.

'I wish you all the happiness in the world.'

The words I spoke aloud resonated deep within me.

Realizing I meant them from the bottom of my heart filled me with happiness.

Thank you. Thank you, Inashiro-san.

I held the letter tightly to my chest.

～

That evening, I sat on the couch, clutching my smartphone, torn between whether to reach out to Yoji or not.

He had contacted me several times, saying he had news to share.

137

I wondered if it was finally time to suggest we meet.

But what could I possibly say, and how?

I opened up the LINE chat screen, unsure of how to start, when suddenly my phone rang.

I nearly dropped the smartphone but managed to catch it before it hit the floor.

It was Yoji.

Holding my chest with one hand, I answered with the other.

'H–hello?'

'Oh, Chiharu! I'm glad you picked up. Are you home now?'

His voice was bright and cheerful.

'Yeah,' I replied.

'I just finished my last meeting for the day. I was getting on a train when I remembered you'd moved somewhere not too far from here.'

He mentioned the name of the train station.

'If you're feeling up it, how about coffee? It won't take long.'

My chest was pounding.

But my heart was already set.

I told him the name of a cafe at the station and asked him to wait for me there.

～

It had only been a month, but it felt as though we hadn't seen each other in years.

He had taken a seat by the window. His hair was freshly trimmed, his bangs shorter than usual.

Even a small change like that made me realize how closely I'd been watching him. Although I was a jumble of emotions, being with him still felt comfortable to me, like being with a childhood friend.

He casually mentioned some updates from work, like how the florist we usually used was opening a second store.

After chatting a while over tea, Yoji straightened up, his face turning serious.

'Listen, I have some news,' he said.

I set my teacup down on the saucer.

I sat up and listened.

Okay, I'm ready to hear it.

Tell me what you have to say.

'I'm getting married. To Sumie. And . . . we're having a baby.'

Yoji was practically beaming, his joy almost impossible to contain.

Ah, I knew it.

Suddenly, tears were rolling down my cheeks.

Yoji looked taken aback, seemingly at a loss for words.

Seeing the look on his face, I realized he had no idea how I felt about him, and a conflicted mix of disappointment and relief washed over me.

As he sat there, confused, I gave him a smile through my tears.

'I'm happy for you. I knew you two were seeing each other.'

I put on a brave face, and deep down, I felt genuinely happy for him. It was an odd feeling.

Yoji let out a sigh of relief.

'Oh, so the secret's out, huh? Anyway, I'm glad you're happy.'

He smiled, his face suddenly like a little boy's.

That's what I loved about him—that innocence bordering on obliviousness.

I had been so afraid of the 'news', so sure I didn't want to know, but now that I had, I felt surprisingly calm.

All the anxious thoughts that had terrified me until now.

I had felt so sorry for myself.

But was that really it?

'Are you eating?' Yoji asked.

'A little at a time,' I answered, nodding.

'Well, then, this is for you.'

He reached into his bag and took out some cookies from Angelica, a pastry shop near the office, with cookies that were so good that you had to line up early in the morning just to buy them.

He must have remembered that I bought them on special occasions or when I needed a little cheering up.

'I wasn't sure if it would be okay to give you food while you're recovering, but I knew you liked these.'

'Thanks, they're great.'

'I'm glad we could meet today. I really wanted you to be the first to know.'

As I looked at Yoji, his eyes were no longer bashful or hesitant. They were serious.

He'd said he happened to be in the neighbourhood after finishing a meeting, but that was a lie. He must have known there was a chance he could see me if work took him this way, so he had brought the cookies with him.

Yoji . . .

He valued me as a colleague and a friend. Finally, I understood, and for the first time, I felt like I could believe it.

I had been too scared to confront what Yoji thought of me and had been blocking it out with my paranoid thoughts.

Even though we weren't lovers, my heart was full knowing that I had become special to him in this way. I was also relieved to know that I could feel this way.

I looked at Yoji. 'Thanks for sharing the big news with me first.'

Those words were from the heart. For now, that was enough.

It was still too soon for me to celebrate the couple without feeling an ache in my chest. I touched my ear, deciding to stop making myself miserable. I would take the time I needed to rest and recover properly.

'Congratulations,' I said. 'But you owe me all-you-can-eat yakiniku for making me listen to your mushy talk, okay?'

Yoji scratched his head, groaning. 'What?'

I'll make sure you treat me plenty, so get ready.

I imagined that day and smiled.

If I took care of my mind and body while imagining enjoyable moments, maybe I could heal and restore myself, just like my father's suit had been brought back to its original form.

No doubt I had an extraordinary imagination.

And if I could use that imagination to expand my capacity for empathy and kindness, maybe I could learn to love others—and myself—a little more honestly.

4

Yuya's Leg

I left the house as usual, calling out, 'I'm going now,' and then stopped outside the big house with the fence.

I scanned my surroundings. No one was around.

I was standing near a garage just out of sight from the street.

I pulled out a pain relief patch from my school backpack. It was one I'd swiped from the medicine box at home. I took off my right shoe and sock and stuck the patch on my ankle.

It was November, the mornings were already cold, and my body flinched slightly at the cool sensation of the patch against my skin.

I looked around again to make sure no one was watching, then put my shoe back on and started walking.

I hopped slightly on one leg, even though my ankle didn't hurt at all.

~

When my dad, whose job frequently required him to travel between Tochigi and Tokyo, got reassigned to the main office, he decided it might finally be possible to settle in Tokyo for good, so he decided to buy a condo.

'Will you be okay transferring to a new school, Yuya?' my mum asked, worried for me, but I didn't think anything of it.

I didn't expect a whole lot from school life to begin with.

I didn't have any close friends or anything I was passionate about, so it would probably be the same no matter where I went.

When I told her I'd be fine, my mum looked relieved, and she started looking for a house with my dad.

While I was at school, they had decided on a new five-storey condominium called Advance Hill.

'The only available unit was on the fourth floor. It's got a great hilltop view,' my mum said dreamily once the contract was signed.

I don't know, but was buying a condo really something to get so excited about?

Sure, a new home was nice. But it was a little smaller than the rental apartment in Tochigi, and the view wasn't the green forest my mum had raved about. It was more like an artificial landscape with lots of houses spread out below.

Of course, since I didn't care either way, it wasn't really a problem. And so, just as I was about to start the fourth grade, I also became the new kid at school.

As expected, my new life was a drag—nothing to get excited or sad about.

But if there was one thing that annoyed me about the school, it was that there were way too many events.

There seemed to be some kind of event every month, each one announced with a clear purpose that the principal would explain at morning assembly, emphasizing just how much it would contribute to our personal growth.

There were the usual sports days and field trips, as well as community-building activities like neighbourhood clean-ups, overnight camping trips, and rice-planting and harvesting to teach us to be thankful for our food.

And the main event for this month—November—was the Ekiden relay race.

I never really got into sports, so the whole thing was a drag.

It soon turned out not everyone had to participate. Instead, three runners would be chosen from each class, and the relay would be a team competition with mixed groups from all six grades. This race had three goals: improving stamina, creating bonds across grade levels and developing a supportive spirit.

Well, okay, then.

Leaving the goal of improving stamina to the runners, and creating bonds across grades to everyone else, I figured I could focus on supporting the others. Even though it still seemed like a drag, I didn't mind cheering and waving from the sidelines.

I figured the fast kids would get picked right away, leaving me free and clear.

And then, something unexpected happened.

Only two students volunteered from the whole fourth-grade class.

Takasugi and Morimura—both were super-fast. Since they'd done really well in the relay in the September sports festival, maybe the other kids were hesitant to compete with them.

'Then we'll draw lots tomorrow. I'll make the slips,' Ms Makimura, our homeroom teacher, said cheerfully.

This drew a chorus of dissatisfied groans from the class.

Ms Makimura ended homeroom without a second thought.

Our teacher was young, cheerful and a bit pushy. Drawing lots seemed fair to all, though I definitely thought luck was just naturally unfair.

I was terrible at rock-paper-scissors, and the vending machine never gave me the capsule toy I wanted. That was why I knew some bad luck was coming my way.

What if I drew the unlucky lot? Just thinking about it made my body tremble. I barely ate my dinner and couldn't sleep.

No way. Please, no.

I detest running.

I was slow. I didn't have a shred of stamina.

Maybe running was fun for the fast kids, but for me, it was nothing but torture. There was no way I wanted to be the only one struggling, gasping for air.

The next morning, I made up my mind.

I'll pretend I sprained my foot. Yeah, that's what I'll do.

After breakfast, I waited for my mum to go out on to the balcony to hang the laundry and then opened the medicine box.

I pulled out a pain relief patch and shoved it into my school backpack.

'I'm going now,' I called, as I headed out the door.

'Have a good day!'

Good, she didn't seem to notice that I'd taken the patch.

As soon as I left the house, I stuck the patch on

my right ankle and started walking to school, giving it my best limp.

~

During morning homeroom, Ms Makimura set a box on the teacher's desk.

'I'll bring this around the classroom, so you can each draw a slip. Wait until everyone has one, and we'll open them together.'

Ms Makimura went around to our desks, her yellow skirt fluttering. Reluctantly, everyone stuck their hands in the box and pulled out a slip of paper.

As Ms Makimura drew closer to my desk, I felt as if my heart might jump out of my mouth.

Would she believe my excuse? Or should I leave it to luck and put my hand in the box?

The box was thrust in front of me.

'Um . . .'

My voice stumbled out of my dry throat.

Ms Makimura fixed her large eyes on me.

I forced out the excuse I had prepared for why I couldn't draw a lot.

'Yesterday, I sprained my ankle on my way home

from school. I twisted it pretty bad, so I have to take it easy for a while. I'm not sure if my ankle will be better in time for the relay race, so . . .'

'What, *really*?'

Ms Makimura's face shifted slightly.

Was she suspicious or just concerned? I couldn't tell.

As I fell silent, my face burning, a voice came from behind me.

'Oh, so that's why you were limping this morning.'

It was Suguru, sitting diagonally behind me.

We weren't really friends or anything. To be honest, I didn't like him very much.

He always wore a goofy grin, his hair was mussed up, and you could never tell what he was thinking.

But his words made me feel braver.

I quickly pulled down my sock to show Ms Makimura the patch on my ankle and twisted my face as if in pain.

'Well, that's too bad.'

Ms Makimura took back the box and moved on to the next student.

Thanks, Suguru! You saved me. I'll return the favour by praying you don't draw the unlucky lot.

I don't know if it was because I prayed for him, but the one who ended up drawing the unlucky lot was Suguru.

On Ms Makimura's cue, we all opened our slips, and Suguru cried, 'Aw, darn! It's me!' then giggled.

Everyone knew Suguru wasn't the athletic type. Takasugi and Morimura exchanged worried glances, but what was decided was decided.

Anyway, that was supposed to be the end of the Ekiden issue.

At least, that's what I thought.

~

How could this have happened?

After hopping around on my right leg for two days, it had started to actually hurt.

Even though I had totally made up the story about spraining it, it felt like my ankle was genuinely swelling.

Every time I put my right foot down, it throbbed and, to my surprise, the pain spread all the way up to my knee.

Okay, now I was really scared.

153

What if something was really wrong with my leg? What if I couldn't walk anymore?

I felt like I was being punished somehow. Maybe God was angry with me.

Worried, I told my mum that I had fallen and twisted my ankle while walking, and now it hurt.

Another lie. The pain, though, was real.

'Did you sprain it? Do you want to put a patch on it?' my mum asked, unconcerned. I shook my head.

I already knew the patch from the medicine box wouldn't help.

'I don't know. It's not just my ankle. My whole right leg hurts.'

My mum's expression grew serious, and she immediately checked to see if the nearby hospital had an orthopedic department and then took me there right away.

After a quick consultation and an X-ray, a grumpy-looking doctor glanced at the images, without even looking at my leg. 'Doesn't seem to be anything wrong with it,' he said. 'It's probably just growing pains. The pain isn't constant, but only lasts a few hours a day, right?'

When he put it like that, I wasn't so sure.

My leg hurt when I walked or crouched; not so much when I was watching TV, but sometimes it hurt when I tried to sleep.

'Stay off it for a while. I'll prescribe you some heating pads.'

That was the end of the examination. I guess my leg just needed warming?

I took a long bath and applied a heating pad, but it didn't seem to help.

My mum said, 'That doctor might have been a bit careless,' and the following week, looked for another hospital.

She found a privately run orthopedic clinic with positive online reviews, just a train stop away. We decided to get a second opinion.

This time, the doctor was pretty cheerful. After taking some X-rays and confirming that nothing was wrong with the bone, he examined my leg, bending and flexing it, and asked where and how it hurt.

'It's anserine bursitis.'

He wrote the words down on a paper on the desk.

He explained that 'anserine' referred to the inner

side of the knee, where the tendons had become irritated and inflamed.

'It's a common condition for athletes who push themselves too hard. You have to ice it properly, okay?'

I was even more confused.

Did he say 'athletes'? As far as I remembered, I hadn't trained for anything.

Besides, the previous doctor had given me heating pads, and now this one was ordering ice. What was I supposed to believe?

I left the hospital in silence.

It seemed my mum was just as unsettled as I was. We headed home in low spirits.

When we arrived at our train stop, she gasped as though she'd remembered something.

'We need to stop at the cleaners. I have to pick up your father's shirts.'

I followed her, and we ended up walking down a backroad I'd never been down before towards an old house. On the ground floor was a store called Sunrise Cleaning.

When my mum slid open the glass door, an

old lady was sitting behind the counter chatting with a long-haired woman who was probably a customer.

The old lady greeted us, causing the customer to turn around.

'Oh,' my mum said, recognizing her and smiling.

'Hello.' The woman smiled back.

She seemed familiar. I was pretty sure she lived in our building. She looked around the same age as Ms Makimura.

'This is Niizawa-san's daughter, Chiharu-chan. Niizawa-san is an officer in the homeowners' association with us. Say hello, Yuya.'

'Hello.'

I bowed my head, and the woman, Chiharu-chan, gave me a warm smile.

My mum walked through to the counter, pulled out a claim ticket from her wallet, and handed it to the old lady.

The lady stood up from behind the counter and asked, 'Yuya-kun, is it? What grade are you in?'

'Fourth grade.'

'Then that would make you ten years old. Only

ten years since you were born! I'm going to be eighty this year. Ten years to me seems like yesterday.'

She laughed and disappeared into the back to get my father's shirts. When she came back, she lifted her chin in my direction.

'Did you hurt your leg?'

She must have noticed the way I was walking.

My mum saw me fidgeting and jumped in: 'I honestly don't know what it is. He complained of pain in his leg, so I took him to two hospitals, but we don't know what's causing it.'

The lady handed my mum several shirts wrapped in plastic. 'You should go see Kabahiko,' she said.

'Kabahiko?'

'If you touch Kabahiko on the same part as the bit of your body that hurts, miracles of miracles, you'll be healed.'

Hearing this made my heart flutter.

It was the first feeling of excitement I had since moving to this place.

Who was Kabahiko? I wondered. Would he be able to heal my leg?

'They call him Healing Kabahiko.' The old lady raised her finger and gave Chiharu-san a quiet nudge.

Chiharu-san smiled awkwardly, 'Because Kaba-hiko sounds like *hippo*.'

My mum clapped and burst out laughing.

Chiharu-san laughed, too. 'I'd be happy to take you to him. Kabahiko has helped me.'

And so, the three of us left Sunrise Cleaning together.

~

We walked down the promenade that led to a bunch of apartment buildings.

The sun was beginning to set, flooding the area in a dreamlike glow. It felt as if I were being invited into a secret forest, and I became all tingly with anticipation.

'Over there.'

Chiharu-san pointed to a tiny park surrounded by apartment buildings. The words 'Hinode Park' were engraved on a big rock at the entrance.

Chiharu-san walked further into the park.

I followed her to the swing set and spotted the hippo in the corner of the playground.

'Oh, it's an animal ride.' My mum let out a deflated laugh.

It was one of those animal-shaped rides you see in playgrounds.

It didn't have footrests or springs, just a hippo you could sit on and ride.

There it sat all alone, with its plump body and mouth stretched into a lazy grin.

The orange paint was chipped in places and the blacks of its eyes had turned white in parts, making him look like he was laughing and crying at the same time.

'So you just touch the part you want to make better, right?' My mum approached Kabahiko and reached underneath towards the underside of his belly. She gave it a rub.

'Does your stomach hurt?' I asked her, a bit worried.

She chuckled and waved her hand. 'No, no, I've just put on some weight and can't fit into my favourite skirt. It might be hard to make me thin, but maybe Kabahiko could make me the size I used to be.'

She stood up and looked down at Kabahiko with a grin. 'What a silly face.' It didn't seem like she really believed the hippo could do anything about her flabby stomach.

But something told me there was something special hidden inside Kabahiko's body.

It was just a playground ride that couldn't speak or move, but I had a feeling it could comfort me somehow.

'You said Kabahiko helped you, too?' my mum asked Chiharu-san.

She nodded. 'Yes, I've been taking time off from work for some health issues.'

My mum covered her mouth in surprise.

Since Chiharu-san looked so healthy, my mom probably didn't realize her situation was serious enough to take off work. Chiharu-san gave a small smile, 'But I'm much better now and I'll be going back to work soon.'

My mum's expression relaxed. 'I'm happy for you. You must have found a good doctor.'

'Yes, I've been going to the hospital and taking medicine, but that's not all. I've also made changes to my lifestyle, worked on rethinking my mindset, started yoga and begun seeing a chiropractor.'

Chiharu-san turned towards the hippo.

'Kabahiko is a precious presence that accepts me as I am and watches over me. He really does bring blessings.'

I knelt in front of Kabahiko and put my hand on his right hind leg.

The leg, smooth and rounded, felt solid in my hand. I patted it gently, silently praying:

Please, please, heal my leg.

So I can walk without any pain again.

~

Since the day we had drawn lots, I had been sitting out gym class and watching from the sidelines.

I should've been happy to have an excuse to skip gym, but I couldn't bring myself to feel that way.

I must have caught some mysterious illness.

Heating or cooling my leg didn't help. The more I focused on it, the worse the pain seemed to get.

I sat cross-legged in the corner of the school grounds, watching the rest of the class run laps.

Suguru stuck out like a sore thumb.

He ran with his jaw stuck out, arms flailing wildly, bow-legged, and his form was a mess. Despite trying his hardest, he was slow and even less athletic than I was.

But why did he look like he was having so much fun? I didn't get it at all.

After class, as we were heading back to the main building, I overheard Takasugi and Morimura talking as they passed me.

'I can't believe how slow Suguru is. Our relay race will be over before it even starts.'

'He found out we've been training together in the mornings, and he asked to train with us. What do you think?'

'*What?* No way. He won't be able to keep up with us.'

'Yeah, right.'

They *should* train together, I thought. They could teach him the proper form.

At the same time, I could understand where Takasugi and Morimura were coming from.

It was easy to imagine Suguru smiling sheepishly as soon as they turned him down, saying, 'Oh, okay.'

～

A couple of days later, my mum decided to take me to a chiropractor named Isezaki-san.

After Chiharu-san mentioned going to a chiropractor, my mum had asked to be introduced to him. It was a clinic Chiharu-san herself had been introduced to by someone from work.

My mother explained excitedly that the clinic didn't have a website and was mostly known through word of mouth.

We took the train to Yokohama and got off at an unfamiliar station. From there we walked a bit, going by a map, until we found an old hidden-away house with a small sign for Isezaki Chiropractic Clinic.

We rang the bell and a man in a black T-shirt and track pants came out. His long hair was pulled back into a ponytail.

This reserved man was Isezaki-san. As we entered the house, I noticed the faint smell of incense.

The foyer led directly into a tatami room, where a narrow bed with a hole at one end was placed.

After Isezaki-san had a brief chat with my mum, he directed me to lie face down on the bed.

A thin sheet of paper covered the hole. I put my head through it, lying face down on the firm bed.

Isezaki-san examined not my leg but the bones in my neck first. His fingers moved down my spine, stopping at my hip.

Placing his fingers on my body, he asked me several times if it hurt.

I answered truthfully each time, 'No.'

Then he turned to my mum and said, 'There's a waiting area in the next room. Would you mind waiting there?'

'Oh, sure,' she replied.

I turned my head to see what was happening. A young woman appeared and showed my mum to the door, who shot me a brief, worried glance before leaving.

Left alone with the doctor, I was a tiny bit scared.

He wasn't like any of the adults I knew.

Neither my father nor my uncles had this mysterious aura, and he didn't look like a typical doctor.

'Now lie down on your back.'

I nervously lifted my head and rolled over.

My eyes met Isezaki-san's.

He smiled softly, and the gentle creases at the
corners of his eyes made me feel a little more at ease.

He began to examine my leg, bending and twist-
ing my knee. Depending on how he moved it, it
hurt. When I told him so, he nodded and moved my
leg a different way.

Once he had finished examining both legs,
Isezaki-san said, 'Yuya-kun, right now, it seems your
whole body is misaligned.'

'*Misaligned?*' I asked.

'Yep, by favouring one foot, the muscles get
tense, and the stress is unevenly distributed throughout your body. I don't think this is a problem with
just your leg.'

He looked me directly in the eye.

'Your body and heart are closely connected, but
your head sits alone, far away. It might be that your
mind is mistaking the tension in your skin and muscles as pain.'

166

Mistaking?

Was that even possible?

What tension in my muscles and skin?

Feeling pain when there was no pain. What did that even mean?

I had so many questions that I couldn't even speak.

Isezaki-san sat on the stool next to the bed and smiled.

'Maybe there's something your body and heart are resisting, something they really don't want to do.'

Before I could stop myself, I muttered, 'I detest running . . .'

Isezaki-san leaned back and chuckled. 'Yeah, I didn't like it either. P.E. was the worst.'

'Really?'

'But now I like exercising. Stretching in the morning, jogging in the evening—it wasn't until I became an adult that I realized how great it feels to move your body. When I was younger, I was forced to follow rigid routines, so I didn't realize how enjoyable it could be until I was free to do things my own way.'

Isezaki-san spoke slowly as if recalling something.

'The body is always changing, and it can send all kinds of messages. Even the tiniest thing can affect the body in surprising ways, for better or for worse. Once I realized that, I began to take an interest in the body. That's how I came to study osteopathy.'

He stood up and placed his hand on my leg again.

'Today, we'll focus on realigning your body. But remember, your body won't heal overnight, so we'll work on listening to your body.'

Listening to my body . . .

I didn't fully understand.

After he finished adjusting and pressing on different parts of my body, Isezaki-san ran his hand over my legs and said, 'That's all for today. You'll come back next week. I'm going to give you two homework assignments.'

Homework?

He motioned for me to get up from the bed and taught me two exercises to help rebalance my body.

At first, I thought those were my two assignments, but then Isezaki-san turned to me and added, 'The second task is to practise shifting your awareness away from your leg.'

Shifting my awareness?

I stared at him blankly.

He continued, 'If you focus too much on the pain or thinking that your leg might not heal, your mind might send the wrong signal. Sometimes, it's important to redirect your anxious feelings rather than confront them head-on.'

Was that even possible?

I looked down at my feet. I couldn't stop thinking about my worries even when I didn't want to.

'It would be helpful if you could focus on something you find enjoyable. If that's tricky, try focusing on some simple tasks.'

'Like what?'

'Something you do every day without thinking. Like eating, brushing your teeth, taking notes from the blackboard—all kinds of things. The key is to stay present and to focus on one moment at a time.'

As he spoke, he led me to the waiting room.

At this chiropractic clinic, which didn't take X-rays or prescribe medication, all they offered was a small cup of green tea before sending you on your way.

～

The next morning, I woke up a little earlier than usual and decided to take the long way to school. I headed straight to Hinode Park.

To see Kabahiko.

Although nothing that I would consider 'enjoyable' came to mind right away, just thinking about Kabahiko did bring me a sense of relief.

As soon as I arrived at the empty park, I walked straight over to him. It seemed as if Kabahiko looked at me and smiled.

It was as if we'd made a promise to meet.

Just as Isezaki-san had said, going to the chiropractic clinic once didn't make the pain in my leg disappear right away. But I did get a good night's sleep and woke up feeling refreshed.

How do I listen to my body? I wondered.

I didn't like running and didn't want to participate in the relay race. That was true of my body, heart and even mind—they all felt the same way.

I had somehow managed to avoid drawing lots and gotten away with only having to cheer from the sidelines. I didn't have to do anything unpleasant anymore.

Then why is my head tricking me into thinking my leg hurts when it doesn't?

Darn, there I go worrying about my leg again. Shifting my focus away from it is hard.

I crouched down in front of Kabahiko. Patting his right leg, I spoke to him.

'Who knew I hated running this much. I'm a coward and a loser.'

And then, I heard a voice.

'You're not a loser.'

What the!?

Did Kabahiko just say something?

I looked around and saw Suguru standing by the swings.

'You're not a loser for hating running,' he said. 'You can't help not liking something.'

Suguru wiped his nose on the cuff of his jacket. It seemed to be a habit, judging by the crusty stain on his cuff.

'Don't you hate running, too?' I asked, still crouching beside Kabahiko. 'I mean, you don't want to run the relay race, do you?'

Suguru tilted his head thoughtfully. 'Naw, I don't mind.'

'But you're not good at it.'

'Yeah, I'm really slow.'

Right? If you know you're slow, then why doesn't that bother you?

I swallowed the words and asked instead, 'But you'll have to run while everyone is watching you.'

'Huh? Yeah, I guess.' Suguru laughed sheepishly. 'I've never run an Ekiden before. But since I got the chance, I figured I might as well give it a try. Who knows—it might end up being fun, or it might just be really tough. But you won't know unless you try.'

Hearing this felt like a punch in the gut.

I froze, as if I had merged with Kabahiko, unable to speak or move. Suguru suddenly began jogging in place.

'Well, gotta keep running. Solo training, you know. The park's the turnaround point. See you at school!'

With that, Suguru ran out of the park. He was probably taking the long way to school as part of his training.

Alone, with his school backpack strapped to his shoulders.

≈

I finally realized.

What my body and heart hated wasn't the running itself.

It was the idea of everyone seeing me fail.

If I had to run alongside all the fast runners, I would fall behind from the start.

Everyone I was representing would be mad at me, and I'd be laughed at by everyone—not just on the day of the race; my whole school life from then on would be doomed.

That was the story I had convinced myself of.

That was why I had been so desperate to avoid it somehow.

But Suguru wasn't the least bit worried about that. About what everyone would think.

He had accepted the role that no one else wanted without complaint.

Even if he wasn't good at running, he was determined to give his best effort.

He had even noticed me hanging around at the park.

I hadn't understood his strength or kindness, until now.

Pressing my forehead against Kabahiko's body, I burst into tears.

As tears ran down my cheeks, the words tumbled out on their own.

It was as if my heart and body were crying out to Kabahiko.

'All . . . all I could think about was how to get out of running the race. I lied . . . and when it worked, it only made me feel worse.'

I stopped.

What did I just say?

Oh, now I get it.

My body had been tense because I felt guilty for being dishonest.

My mind had it all wrong.

In my heart of hearts, I never wanted to lie. That's right . . .

What I disliked was that side of myself.

~

The next week, I went back with my mum to Isezaki Chiropractic Clinic.

I had completed the two assignments that Isezaki-san gave me for homework.

I did the exercises to realign my body every morning before school and at night after my bath.

As for the second assignment, practising to take my mind off my leg, I focused on some simple tasks, just as Isezaki-san had suggested.

I was amazed. It led to a series of unexpected results.

For example, when I ate, thinking about the ingredients and how the food was prepared made it taste better than before. When I brushed my teeth, focusing on each tooth helped me to brush more carefully. During class, while taking notes from the blackboard, I tried writing as neatly as I could, which made learning the information easier.

Maybe none of this was all that surprising.

Until then, I had eaten what was put in front of me without really thinking about it; I ran my brush quickly over my teeth, barely paying attention; and there were times I hardly looked at the blackboard during class.

That practice of staying in the moment also started to change the way I saw everyday life.

The way my fingers bent when I clipped my nails, the smell of pencil lead, the sound of rain hitting an umbrella—when you focus your attention on the present, you discover so many things you've never noticed before.

In doing so, the time I spent worrying about my leg gradually decreased.

By the time I went to see Isezaki-san again, I wasn't obsessing over my leg anymore. I had been so worried about it before, but now I had forgotten all about my pain. My body felt warm and relaxed.

With just the two of us in the room again, I lay face down while Isezaki-san examined me. After a while, he grunted, 'Good. I'm surprised at how much progress you made in a week. The tension in your body has improved a lot. You're much more relaxed now.'

I looked up at Isezaki-san, smiling proudly. 'Has my leg healed?'

'What?' Isezaki-san chuckled, then nodded. 'Yeah, I'd say it has. Good job.'

'Then, I'm back to normal?'

I need to go thank Kabahiko.

I nuzzled my face back against the hole in the bed, smirking, but Isezaki-san said, 'Not exactly. The human body, after it heals, doesn't necessarily return to the condition before it was injured.'

'*Huh?*'

'The memory and experience of having been ill or injured are imprinted on the body, the heart and the mind. So, after you recover, you're a different person than you were before.'

Confusing.

I lifted my head slightly out of the hole and asked, 'By "different", am I a better or worse person than I was before?'

'That's not for me to decide. I do this work, hoping that it helps people move in a positive direction. At the very least, you've begun to understand things that you didn't before your leg started hurting. I hope that understanding helps you move forward in a positive way.'

Isezaki-san fell silent and continued to press down carefully on my body.

As I felt his fingers on my back, I drifted into thought, wondering what would come after recovery.

～

The next morning, I woke up early again and headed to Hinode Park. After giving my thanks to Kabahiko, I sat astride his back and waited for Suguru.

The swings, the slide, the sandbox and the bench—everything in the tiny park looked old and worn.

How long has this park been here? How old is Kabahiko?

Lost in my thoughts, I began to get cold and gave my arms a rub. Just then, I spotted Suguru running past the bushes bordering the park.

I hopped off Kabahiko.

I headed out of the park and came face to face with Suguru just as he was coming in.

'Hey, Yuya!'

'M–morning.'

'Morning! Funny how we keep meeting here,' he said cheerfully, a little out of breath.

'I waited, thinking you might come here.'

'What? You were waiting for me? How come?'

I squeezed my fist, then looked at him directly.

'So, um, the Ekiden is a week away. Do you want to train for the race with me?'

'With you, Yuya?'

I nodded at Suguru, who stood there, his mouth hanging open in shock.

'I'm not that good at running either, so I can't teach you the proper form or anything . . . but it might be fun to run together.'

Suguru let out a strange hoot and swung his arms in circles.

'Really? That would be awesome!'

Seeing him hopping with excitement, I felt a wave of relief come over me.

I'd been worried that he might be annoyed by my invitation, but I was glad I had worked up the courage to ask.

Suguru stopped swinging his arms and, with a look of concern, asked, 'But is your leg okay? And besides, I thought you said you hated running.'

I answered firmly, 'Yup, I'm recovered now. I'm not the same person I was before.'

~

We decided on a path along the river, slightly off our school route, as our training course. Each morning, we met without our school backpacks, ran our route, then went back home to get ready for school.

We practised together as best we could, discussing things like posture and stride as we continued our training. Whether or not our methods were perfect, we both felt our bodies gradually getting used to running.

And . . . not only that, it was fun! Running alongside Suguru turned out to be more enjoyable than I ever would have imagined.

If I'm honest, there were mornings that week when I would wake up early, while it was still dark outside, and think, *I don't wanna do this*. But meeting up with Suguru and exercising made me feel incredibly happy and good.

The day before the relay race, after we finished our run, Suguru cheered, 'All this training is going to make you super-fast!'

It was so like him to be this positive, and I couldn't help but laugh.

'I sure hope so, even though I won't be participating in the relay race.'

Suguru looked at me, wide-eyed.

'*Huh?* But you're already participating. I mean, you've been great about cheering me on.'

'Oh . . . yeah . . .'

'Totally! Knowing you'll be watching from the sidelines, I'm definitely going to give it my all. You know what's strange? Even though I'm the one running, when I hear someone cheering me on, it feels like I have more strength than just my own.'

He flexed his arms and beamed.

'Thanks, Yuya!'

I felt my chest tighten and could only manage a small nod.

That goes for me, too, Suguru.

I was sure I'd gained even more strength from cheering him on.

~

The day of the Ekiden relay race.

The race was held at the big park near school.

I stood with the squad cheering for my team, shouting with all my might.

The sash was passed from the first-grade runner

to the second, then to the third, and when it reached Takasugi, the fourth-grade runner, our team was in the lead. Our cheers grew louder.

I moved away from the cheering squad and caught a glimpse of Takasugi passing the sash to Suguru.

When Suguru almost fumbled the pass, Takasugi yelled, 'Hey, get it together!'

My palms began to sweat.

You can do it, Suguru!

One of the runners quickly overtook him. Until then, we'd been in the lead. Disappointed murmurs rippled around me.

As Suguru threw his arms and legs forward, I cheered for him so loudly that I thought my throat might tear.

And then it happened. Suguru's legs got all tangled, and he stumbled right in front of me.

He took such a spectacular fall that it almost seemed like a joke. A huge gasp erupted from the crowd—and then, laughter, anger and dismay all mixed together.

Suguru had fallen forward, sprawled on his hands and feet like a frog. His body trembled as he tried desperately to lift himself up.

'Suguru!'

I dashed out from behind the rope and on to the track.

I barely had time to think.

Before I knew it, I was running towards him.

~

When I reached his side, Suguru twisted his body away from me and tried to escape.

'D-don't!'

'Huh?'

This blunt rejection stopping me dead in my tracks, Suguru said, 'If you touch me, I'll be disqualified. I can still keep going.'

Another runner passed us.

Suguru wobbled to his feet and started running again, dragging his injured leg.

I let out a deep breath.

I moved to the edge of the course, staying near the rope, careful not to get in the way of the other runners. Keeping Suguru in the corner of my eye . . .

I started running with him.

Come on, Suguru. You can do it.

I'm right here with you.
Watching.
Cheering right alongside you.
I knew what I was doing was weird.
From the cheering line, I could hear exasperated voices shout, 'What is he doing?' and loud laughter.
I continued to run, keeping pace with Suguru.

I've never run an Ekiden before, Suguru had said. Since he didn't know whether it would be fun or tough, he figured he might as well give it a try and find out.

It's like what the old lady at Sunrise Cleaning had said: we'd only been alive for ten years, and there was so much we didn't know. From here on out, we would probably face all kinds of challenges and feel all sorts of emotions.

We would figure out what we liked, what we didn't, what was fun, and what was painful through trial and error. If we kept shrinking back, worrying about how others saw us, trying not to show the uncool parts of ourselves or avoid being laughed at, we would probably lose sight of what those things even meant.

That was why, from here on out, step by step, I was going to decide who I was.

～

Suguru ran with an odd, unsteady stride, scrapes all over his arms and legs, drool and snot hanging from his chin.

But he was looking straight ahead, a faint smile on his face, and in that moment, I knew he was super-cool.

5

Kazuhiko's Eyes

To see it clearly, I pushed it away.

The functions of the human body were truly strange. As I read the tiny text, which resembled gnats perched on the page, I instinctively pushed the document further away from me.

My hands naturally started moving away about five or six years ago. The small print on my smart-phone screen, restaurant menus, medicine labels and even galley proofs began to blur and appeared to recede further every time I tried to read them.

~

'Mizobata-san, would you check the galleys, please?'

Takaoka, a member of the editorial team, placed a stack of A3 papers on my desk.

A galley proof was a printed version of a publication, formatted as it would appear in the final version, for review.

'Right,' I muttered, giving a half-hearted reply as I picked it up.

It had been thirty years since I started working at Eiseisha, a magazine publisher in Tokyo. After graduating from university, I spent five years in the company's sales department before transferring to the editorial department of a weekly magazine. Ten years ago, the monthly general interest magazine *Laughter* was launched, and I became its editor-in-chief.

Editing a general interest magazine had been my dream since school. Seeing my name, Kazuhiko Mizobata, listed as editor-in-chief on the colophon filled me with pride.

But in recent years, I could no longer push myself as I had when I was younger. Lately, both my body and mind were struggling. Fatigue weighed on me constantly, and I was easily consumed with negativity over the smallest things. In short, I no longer had the ease I once did. Even drinking no longer helped me shake off the tension, and the knots in my shoulders had become chronic.

As December set in and the cold grew harsher, I couldn't get by without wearing thermal underwear. I even began wearing leggings like long johns. My circulation and metabolism worsened and I suffered the cold far more than I used to.

While reading through the galley proofs of the store profiles, something caught my attention, prompting me to call out to Takaoka.

When he approached, I was a bit surprised to see he was only wearing a cotton shirt. If I remembered correctly, Takaoka had just turned thirty. That made him more than twenty years younger than my fifty-two—practically the age of another adult.

He stopped at my desk and with a casual 'What's up?' turned his narrow face towards me. I pointed to a photo in the article.

'This store, Various . . .'

To which he curtly said, 'Not Various . . . it's Variety.'

'Uh . . .'

I misread it. This was happening more frequently of late.

Scowling, I moved the galley slightly further away, and Takaoka let out a small laugh.

'Oh, are your eyes going?'

This guy really has no filter.

When I didn't respond, he said, as if out of some misplaced kindness, 'You ought to take care of that sooner rather than later. When you squint, your face becomes tense and wrinkles start to form.'

Shut up. What do you know?

I first noticed difficulty reading in my mid-forties. My vision was 20/40 in both eyes, but I knew it was getting worse. I worried people might think I was getting old if I suddenly started wearing reading glasses, so I had purchased bifocal contact lenses.

But when I tried them on, seeing up close and far away became even blurrier, making them uncomfortable to wear. Thinking the lenses weren't a good fit for me, I gave up wearing them after the one-week trial period.

I was still able to manage without the lenses. I had no choice but to keep going as long as I could.

I remained silent and Takaoka peered over at the galleys.

'So, what is it?'

'Isn't the photo of the store interior too dark?'

'Oh, that's the vibe they're known for. They're really popular with couples and young people these days.'

His tone seemed to mock the fact I didn't already know that.

It ticked me off. *You're not going to stay young forever!* 'Huh,' I muttered.

Pale, smooth skin. Stylish dress. Media savvy.

Takaoka was easy to talk to and quick on his feet. As much as it pained me to admit it, he was an indispensable member of the editorial department. Ignoring my frown, he said, 'By the way,' with a tilt of his head. 'The latest volume of *Bura-man* is coming out soon.'

He was referring to *Black Manhole* or *Bura-man* for short, a manga published by Eiseisha. A massive hit and the publisher's tentpole title, it won the Ultra Manga Award and was adapted into an anime, which helped its sales soar.

'I'm a big fan,' said Takaoka. 'I'd like to do a

special feature not just on *Bura-man* but on its creator Ryo Sunagawa. Would you mind taking a look at my proposal? It'd sure be nice to meet him.'

'Don't bring such questionable motives into your work,' I said.

Manga creators, writers, celebrities—if you worked in magazine editing, it wasn't unusual to meet a public figure you admired. But pitching features for that reason could lead to bias.

Takaoka cocked his head. 'Is it questionable, though? An editor needs passion, or the article won't be any good.'

Don't talk big, you punk.

I suppressed the urge to snap back at him. *He's only running his mouth because he's young*, I told myself.

Instead, I said, 'Show me what you got, and I'll take a look,' and dropped my gaze back to the galley proofs.

~

By the time I finished work and arrived at my train stop, it was already past 9 p.m. I exited the ticket gate and walked through the nearly deserted shopping arcade.

In April, my wife and I had bought a condominium in a new building.

From its name, Advance Hill, I knew that it was perched on a hill, but the view was even better than I'd imagined.

Though it had cost a pretty sum, I didn't regret choosing a unit on the top floor—the fifth—despite the steep climb up to the building's entrance.

Previously, my wife, Miyako, and I had lived in a rental apartment near work. Although the new place had three bedrooms, like our previous one, the floors and walls were sturdier, and Miyako seemed pleased with the convenience of the kitchen disposer and the package delivery boxes.

Along with our move to a new home, we also welcomed a new member into the family: our cat, Ciao. Miyako had found her from a posting about a rescue cat in need of a home.

She was a grey-striped silver tabby with white legs and belly. She was thought to be around six months old, or roughly ten years in human years. Miyako, who mostly stayed home except for the occasional temporary job, had always wanted to live with a cat.

I emerged from the arcade on to a narrow path and stopped.

Up ahead was a red overhang with the words 'Sunrise Cleaning'.

The building itself was an old two-storey house with the upstairs serving as a residence. The storefront was shuttered, but through the balcony, I could see the light was on upstairs.

Some dingy green curtains were drawn across the closed windows. I pictured the elderly woman who ran the store alone in the tiny house.

Perhaps she was up there watching television. I stared up at the lit room for a moment longer before lowering my gaze and walking on.

I continued down the promenade towards a small park.

A stone slab engraved with the words 'Hinode Park' marked the entrance. It was well into night, and there was no one around.

My eyes met the swing set, slide and sandbox. This rundown playground was where I used to play as a child. The building that housed Sunrise Cleaning had been my childhood home, where I was raised as the only son of the owner, Yukie Mizobata.

I had moved back to the area, inconveniently further away from work, because I was worried about my mother. We had become distant after I finished university and left home.

I had no memory of my father. By the time I was old enough to notice anything, he was already gone. My mother had raised me all on her own.

She was strong-willed, spirited and always talking, always working.

While dependable, she had a way of thinking she was always right.

Although I understood the need for the two of us to support each other through life, I felt trapped by my mother's overbearing and nagging ways.

We fought constantly and always ended up ignoring each other. Things just weren't working out. After I started my job and moved out to live on my own, I became too busy to think about her. Nor were there any signs that she was trying to reach out, and in some ways I felt relieved by that.

When the time came to tell her I was getting married after turning thirty, I brought Miyako to the house for a single visit. Come to think of it, that was the last time I had been home since graduating from university.

Although my mother didn't oppose the marriage, she didn't exactly seem to warm to Miyako either. She barely made eye contact, said very little, only nodding the occasional 'Okay'. Since we didn't have a wedding ceremony, there was no reason to stay in touch, so time simply passed.

What triggered my concern about the future was Miyako's parents.

Two years ago, when her parents were both about to turn eighty, Miyako's older brother and his wife invited them to come live with them. Seeing her parents so overjoyed by the invitation brought to the surface things I had long pretended not to notice.

I couldn't help but picture my mother's face, and the thought of the future weighed on me emotionally.

Until then, my mother was a topic I had avoided with my wife. When I finally opened up about my feelings, Miyako fell silent for a moment, then consented to my mother coming to live with us.

But unlike Miyako's brother and his wife, who

had lived near their parents and saw them regularly, I recognized even bringing up the subject with my mother would be difficult. That was why I had taken the step to buy the condo nearby.

One month before the move-in date, I finally mustered the courage to call my mother.

I told her our new address and even went as far as to say that I was nearby if she needed anything, but she didn't seem at all happy.

On the contrary, she said, 'I don't remember asking,' thereby quashing any desire I had for her move in with us.

I was at a loss for what to do next. The tension between us only grew, and we hadn't spoken since.

The only sense of closeness that purchasing the condo at Advance Hill had brought me was on the occasions Miyako took our clothes to the cleaners and saw my mother. As much as I regretted relying on Miyako for this, the one saving grace was that I could check in on my mother through her. All I managed to do in that time for Miyako was to buy a chestnut cake, a seasonal food sold only in October at a popular pastry shop, for her birthday. It felt completely inadequate. What must she have thought when saw the cake which I had bought as a gesture of both gratitude and apology?

Miyako and I met at Eiseisha. Back when I was still in the sales department, she started working part-time in the editorial department of a women's magazine. She was a university student, four years younger than me.

She handled detailed tasks meticulously and had a reserved, always calm demeanour that I found appealing. She often wore dresses with floral patterns and blouses with lace at the cuffs, both of which suited her.

After graduating from university, she worked at an interior design company, which she left when she married me. Now, in her late forties, she wore her long, black hair in a single braid, giving her a youthful appearance.

However, the calm and reserved demeanour I admired could sometimes come across as reticent and inscrutable. What seemed like anger might simply have been fatigue; dismayingly, the opposite could also be true. No doubt, my own unperceptiveness contributed to misunderstandings. The excitement and intimacy we once shared when we were both young had long faded, and we rarely even looked at each other anymore.

Then there was the issue of my mother. I couldn't shake the guilt that Miyako might end up being more involved with my mother than I had ever been, after years of avoiding contact with her.

It made me feel insecure about so many things all at once.

I stood in front of the hippo ride next to the swing set.

It was a simple, orange-coloured hippo without any footrests or spring mounts.

Patches of paint had peeled off, exposing the concrete beneath. The eyes, once painted black, had turned white in places, giving them a teary look. Still, the mouth was spread into a smile, which added to its comical appearance.

I gently placed my hand on his round head.

You're still here.

What are you crying about?

You used to be shiny orange back in the day. Your eyes were completely black, not teary like they are now.

As I gazed at the hippo's tearful expression, my thoughts wandered to a distant memory.

Healing Kabahiko.

One time, the class bully had struck me on the back, leaving me crying. Around the same time, the hippo ride was installed in the park.

That was when my mother had held up a finger and said, 'This little guy came here just for you, Ka-zuhiko. He's your number-one ally. He has incredible powers. If you touch him in the same spot where you're hurting, he'll heal you. They call him Healing Kabahiko.'

I wasn't sure what it all meant, and my mother flashed a grin. 'Get it? Because Kaba-*hiko* rhymes with *hippo*.'

I burst out laughing. My mother hugged me tightly and said, 'It's going to be okay!'

Even as a grade-schooler, I knew my mother had made the story up. Still, I sensed an overflowing amount of love, and it had made me happy. From that moment on, Kabahiko became my companion.

But Kabahiko and I had both grown old.

And here I am, back to repair my relationship with my mother.

Everyone grew old eventually.

Time gave us many things, but it also took things away.

It didn't seem fair. Up until now, I had overcome everything through hard work. I did not like being bullied, so I studied hard and earned good grades. I knew our family wasn't well off, so I attended university on a scholarship. From getting a job at my top-choice company to proposing to Miyako, I'd overcome every challenge through hard work and effort.

But now, swallowed up by the relentless passage of time, a force I couldn't outwit no matter what, I was left stunned.

I had grown more forgetful, and my legs began to ache from going up and down the stairs. When I was tired, my ears rang, and when I went to the dentist about a toothache caused by a cavity, he told me that it was due to gum deterioration.

When you got sick or injured, there was always the hope that proper treatment could make you better. But when the cause was ageing, there was nothing you could do. I no longer had the energy or stamina to fend off the various ailments creeping into my body.

I patted Kabahiko's eyes.

If only my ageing eyes could go back to the way they were . . .

And if only my relationship with my mother could go back to how it was when I was a kid.

'Do something, Kabahiko.'

The hippo looked back at me as though he was struggling to smile through his pain.

A pang of sadness washed over me as I pulled my hand away from him.

～

A few days later, Miyako told me my mother was coming for a visit.

Though I had no idea how Miyako had managed to invite her, it was decided my mother would come for dinner after closing the store.

Was it some kind of blessing from Kabahiko?

The thought briefly crossed my mind.

'Which do you think she'd like better—chirashi sushi or yakiniku?' Miyako asked beforehand, but I couldn't answer.

I remembered my mother preferred meat over fish, but her tastes might have changed. I didn't even know that.

I was nervous. If there was even the slightest chance of repairing our relationship, I would suggest she come live with us. Would I be able to bring it up tactfully? I played with Ciao while I waited for her to arrive.

While Ciao usually snuggled up next to Miyako, she seemed to see me more as a playmate and was a bit friskier around me.

She would nibble on me or suddenly pounce when I least expected it. Those were the times that made her irresistible, of course.

Like all cat owners, I was convinced we had the most adorable cat in the world. I couldn't forget, just this morning, how adorably she'd crawled into my futon. I ran my fingers gently over her paws, recalling the sweet moment.

Why was she so perfectly formed? The immaculately triangular ears, the round eyes, the gentle slope of her back—she was perfect in every way. And then, without any warning, she would nuzzle her body against mine. Other times, she would sit quietly by the wall, ignoring me, and swat at the curtains swaying in the wind.

After I'd folded the laundry, she would playfully bat at it, then knead her front paws into it—what was that all about? She was a cute little girl.

I was feeling her smooth toe beans with my fingers, when the intercom rang. I jumped to my feet, causing Ciao to arch her back in surprise.

On the intercom screen was my mother standing outside the building entrance. Miyako answered, 'Hi,' and pressed the unlock button.

I sat on the couch, feigning calm, and opened a newspaper. Ciao immediately jumped next to me.

Soon the doorbell chimed. Miyako went into the foyer to answer it.

I tried to act casual, keeping my eyes on the newspaper. Only the headlines were large enough to make out.

My mother walked into our living room. Her hair was cut short, a full head of silver hair approaching white.

Ciao jumped down from the couch.

'Oh, you have a cat,' my mother remarked.

Before we made eye contact, her attention was drawn to the cat.

'If you're uncomfortable, I can put her in the other room if you'd like,' Miyako offered, holding a hanger in one hand and extending her other hand towards my mother.

My mother took off her coat and handed it to her.

'The shop is known for being open year-round, so thankfully, that keeps us quite busy. I would take even a cat's help if I could.'

Her response was oddly off the mark, and her voice unnaturally loud.

Startled perhaps by a voice she didn't recognize, Ciao scampered away to a corner.

My mother pursed her lips and let out a small snort.

Miyako hung my mother's coat on the hanger and remarked, 'Oh, this embroidery is lovely.'

The collar was adorned with an embroidered leaf design in a gradation of green. Against the grey coat, the embroidery stood out vividly.

'Isn't it?' my mother answered, looking somewhat pleased. Guided by Miyako, she took a seat at the four-person table.

A hot pot for mizutaki was set out on the table.

'There's meat and fish. And plenty of vegetables.'

The choice to make hot pot was Miyako's thoughtful way of letting my mother eat what she liked.

The conversation stalled for a while as the ingredients were tossed into the pot. When it finally came to a boil, Miyako spoke up.

'Did you do the embroidery on your coat yourself?'

My mother nodded.

'It got caught on a nail and tore a hole.'

I glanced at the coat hanging on the wall hook.

'You patched the hole on your own?'

Miyako chuckled at my choice of words. 'It's called visible darning. Instead of blending the stitching into the fabric, you purposely repair the hole with colourful thread.'

'Visible darning, huh?'

It was the first time I had heard the phrase. It had been a while since I didn't know something, not because I couldn't keep up with the younger generation, but simply because it was unfamiliar.

My mother served herself some nappa cabbage from the pot.

'It's stylish, isn't it? In the past, everyone used to look after things they cherished, stitching up the places that needed mending. Now with the world overflowing with products, people just throw things away at the first sign of wear and tear.'

'You're right,' I said. 'Especially when the damage is on a noticeable spot like the collar.'

'It's just a little adjustment, I suppose. I actually like it even more with the addition of the leaf.'

The conversation was flowing.

Perhaps the steam from the hot pot was warming her heart.

Feeling a little more relaxed, I decided to speak the words I had been preparing.

'Why don't you come over for a meal from time to time? It must be tough doing everything yourself all the time.'

My mother paused her chopsticks before answering, 'It isn't tough, actually. You've always had a knack for assuming, haven't you?'

A chill swept through my chest. I fell silent.

You're the one always making assumptions! You've always had a special knack for upsetting people.

Just as I thought the conversation was going well,

now this. Suddenly, I felt like getting up from the table and going into the other room. But I knew I couldn't do that, considering all the effort Miyako put into arranging dinner.

A tense silence settled between us. Only the peaceful bubbling of the hot pot filled the room.

Ciao darted between the legs of the dining table and leapt onto a cushion.

My mother looked down, rolling the chicken meatball on her dish with chopsticks, then muttered, 'Besides, you have a cat in the house.'

A stabbing pain pierced the depths of my chest, my mother's irritated expression cutting into me.

'I hate cats,' she went on. 'They scratch, they bite and they're fickle. Besides, they never seem to like me. They don't grow attached at all, so I just can't find them cute.'

That was the last straw.

How dare she talk badly about Ciao? I lost it and raised my voice.

'Here I am, trying to meet you halfway, and this is the attitude you're taking?'

The crease between my mother's brows deepened.

'Kazuhiko, I don't need you meddling in my business!'

Things were only getting worse. I knew this wasn't working, but I couldn't stop myself.

'You're the one being stubborn and childish!' I shot back.

'Since when did you get so high and mighty?' she snapped.

Miyako said nothing, only watched as the argument escalated.

'This is ridiculous. I'm leaving!' my mother shouted and abruptly rose from the table—

—Only to sway and collapse on the floor.

~

Miyako and I hastily called an ambulance, though even after my mother was rushed to a nearby hospital, as soon as she regained consciousness she insisted, 'I'm telling you I'm fine,' with her usual sharp tongue.

Despite her constant complaints, she seemed to have acknowledged her frailty. Grumbling the entire time, she underwent blood, urine and CT tests, and spent an hour on the bed hooked up to an IV while waiting for the results.

After some more conversation, my mother admitted she had begun to have dizzy spells while working.

The doctor concluded it was anemia and exhaustion. Thankfully, there were no signs of any major issues. We were relieved nothing serious was found, though the doctor frowned upon hearing that she ran the store alone year-round.

'That's too much to handle at your age.'

Although it was difficult to tell through his mask, I realized the doctor was quite young. He was probably around Takaoka's age. He seemed to be managing the night shift in the emergency room with ease.

'Age . . . age . . . stop making it sound like that's a bad thing,' my mother muttered.

She didn't sound angry, just sad. And that made me feel even sadder.

That's right. Growing older isn't a bad thing.

Still, Mum, some things do become difficult.

I feel it myself now, even in my fifties. You've done so well at eighty to make it this far.

I wanted to say this to her, but I swallowed my words. She'd just accuse me of meddling again.

With some colour back in her face, she was cleared to go home. Miyako suggested she stay over at our place for the night, but, of course, my mother refused. We called a taxi, and when we arrived at Sunrise Cleaning, my mother gave Miyako a slight bow before disappearing through the back entrance.

That was yesterday. Today, unable to concentrate on anything, I left work early and stopped by Sunrise Cleaning in the evening.

The shop was open. Business as usual. From a distance, I could see my mother chatting cheerfully with a customer. Without stepping inside, I turned on my heels and walked away.

The sun was setting, but it was still just after 5 p.m. I headed towards Hinode Park.

From the entrance, I noticed a boy with a black school backpack squatting in front of Kabahiko.

The sight of the boy's back reminded me of myself when I was in elementary school, and I felt my chest tighten with emotion.

I used to talk to Kabahiko like that, too, on my

way back from school. Kabahiko would listen to anything.

I could confide in him about the bullies in my class, about getting a perfect score on a test, about what it might be like to have a father.

I wondered whether Kabahiko was a companion to the boy, too, and if so, I was happy for him.

The boy patted Kabahiko's rear leg several times, then got up. When he turned around, his face looked familiar.

Just as I realized he lived in my building, his eyes caught mine.

I called out to him. 'You're from Advance Hill.'

The boy also seemed to recognize me and gave me a shy smile and a bow. Somehow, that put me at ease and I walked over.

To avoid alarming him, I introduced myself. 'Um, I'm Mizobata from the fifth floor.'

The boy nodded slightly.

'I'm on the fourth floor. I'm Yuya Tachihara.'

His dark, unwavering eyes looked directly at me.

His whole life was ahead of him.

He would keep growing and learn to do more and more things.

You can become anything you want, Yuya-kun.

'Were you talking to the hippo?' I asked, and Yuya-kun's shoulders shook with delight.

'His name is Kabahiko,' he said.

'*What?*' My eyes widened. *How did he know his name?*

Before I could find the words, he gently placed his hand on the hippo's head.

'He's amazing. There's a legend that if you touch the part of his body where you're hurting, Kabahiko will heal it.'

Heal it? Wait, that's . . .

Lifting a finger, Yuya-kun said, 'They call him—'

Before I knew it, I jumped in, finishing the line for him: 'Healing Kabahiko!' Then I added the explanation: 'Because Kaba-*hiko* sounds like *hippo.*'

Yuya-kun broke into a sunny smile. 'So, you know about it, too!'

Know about? I'd always assumed it was just a story my mother made up.

'Where did you hear it, Yuya-kun?'

'From the lady at Sunrise Cleaning. She said Kabahiko has helped a lot of people. The lady on the third floor had something wrong with her ears, but she said she's ready to go back to work after New Year's.'

I had to laugh. So that's it.

That's amazing. You're a legend, Kabahiko—at least, within the small world of Sunrise Cleaning's regular customers.

I recalled Yuya-kun had been squatting in front of Kabahiko. 'Is your leg hurting you? You were touching Kabahiko there earlier.'

Yuya-kun shook his head emphatically.

'No, my leg's all better now. Sometimes, I come here to pet Kabahiko, wishing I could make my own decisions about the path I want to walk.'

He was wise beyond his years. Nothing like the crybaby I used to be.

'I'm glad your leg is feeling better.'

Yuya-kun thought for a bit. 'Did you know your body doesn't go back to exactly how it was after recovering from an illness or injury? That's what the chiropractor told me.'

I felt a pang of sadness inside me.

He was right. It was the natural order of things, an inevitability for all living things.

Even an elementary school kid understood that.

There was no going back—to the youthful body I once had, to the relationship I left behind when I bolted out of my childhood home.

Both my mother and I suffered for not being able to fully accept this truth.

As I dropped my eyes, Yuya-kun continued, 'Things may not go back to how they were, but with experience and memories, you can become something different from what you were before.'

Become something different?

It felt as though my world had become a tiny bit brighter. Next to Yuya-kun, Kabahiko was gazing up at me with his dewy eyes and warm grin.

If there was a way for us to face each other, even if it wasn't the same as when I was a child . . .

Maybe I needed to reach out to her, even if it meant risking another fight that could freeze the air between us.

I wouldn't cry and cling to her as I did back then, and she wouldn't wrap me in her arms like a small child anymore. Of course not. Time had carried us forward to a different version of ourselves from the past.

Experience and memories.

215

Between the two of us, my mother and I had more than enough—plenty, in fact.

~

I waved goodbye to Yuya-kun and retraced my steps back to Sunrise Cleaning.

I didn't know what I would say to her—only that I had to see her. That was all for now.

I saw my mother sitting in front of the store. I started to quicken my steps towards her, thinking she might be feeling ill again, but stopped in my tracks. I realized she was gazing at something, a soft smile on her lips.

When I followed her gaze, I saw a stray black cat.

It was eating cat food from a dirty, green dish.

The dish looked familiar. It was an old ceramic one that I frequently used to see on the dining table when I was still living upstairs. Which meant that my mother had bought the cat food?

I found myself staring at her in puzzlement as she gazed kindly at the cat.

And she said she hated cats! *Liar.*

But then a realization hit me, and I drew a deep breath.

To see it clearly, she pushed it away.

Deep down, she actually likes cats.

That was why she kept her distance, looking upon the cat so tenderly.

They scratch, they bite . . .

That was what she'd said, her face full of frustration and sadness.

Wait, I get it now.

She was scared.

Scared of those small claws, and those tiny fangs. Of not being liked.

≈

Maybe my mother had a habit of distancing herself from the people she needed.

Because she was afraid of placing her hopes in others, scared of hurting both herself and them.

Maybe even with my father.

Suddenly, she looked up at me.

'Oh, Kazuhiko. It's you.'

She got up slowly as I walked over to her. This time she didn't wobble, but her face seemed a little downcast as she muttered, 'I'm thinking of closing the shop.'

'Is it that time already?'

I glanced at my watch. It was about 6 p.m.

'No, I meant before the end of the year. I have to admit, passing out in front of you and Miyako-san really shook me. I shudder at the thought of something like that happening in front of customers.'

She looked up at the store name on the red overhang.

Close the store. She was planning to shutter it for good.

As I was struck speechless, my mother switched back to her usual assertive tone. 'Don't worry. I won't be a bother to you. I do have some savings tucked away.'

Her willful voice snapped me back to my senses.

'Who said anything about taking care of you?'

'Oh, well, okay,' she answered curtly, sliding the door closed.

Instantly, I put a hand on the door. She glanced at me suspiciously, making me avert my eyes.

'I, uh . . . came by to grab a book.'

'A book?'

'On my bookshelf. Information I need for work.'

It was a complete lie.

I took a step inside, wedging the toe of my shoe into the doorframe.

My mother grunted and didn't press me any further. Instead, she went behind the counter and began tidying up.

The area behind the counter was a workspace.

Sewing tools and an ironing board cluttered the table, and next to them, a white cloth draped over heavy machinery.

Plastic wrapping and machines for pressing shirts or removing stains, once essential to the store's operation, now sat unused—relics from when my mother and father used to manage the laundry business together.

After some hesitation, I went back behind the counter into the narrow hallway, slipped off my shoes, and climbed the stairs. Why hesitate? This was my childhood home, after all.

The air felt familiar. The smell of damp wood.

The creaky stairs. They brought back distant memories, stirring a swirl of emotions I couldn't quite name.

For the first time in years, I stepped into the second-floor residence. At the top of the stairs was the kitchen.

I flicked the switch, and the lights blinked a couple of times before turning on.

On the stove was a small pot. I lifted the lid and found a small portion of stewed eggplant inside, limp and cold. Probably last night's leftovers.

Ignoring the squeal of my stomach, I put the lid back on and went into my room.

The six-tatami-mat room was exactly the same as I remembered, frozen in time.

The grey curtains, the steel bookcase, and the pipe-frame bed. How ecstatic I'd been when I got the study desk upon entering elementary school. I used it until I graduated from university.

My eyes stopped on the issues of *Lucas*, a manga magazine I used to buy every release day, still lining the shelves of the bookcase. I reached out to grab one when I noticed something.

There was no dust on the bookcase, even though it had been years since I left home.

Has Mum been cleaning my room?

I heard the shutters closing downstairs.

After a few seconds, I heard my mother coming slowly up the stairs. Her footsteps weren't as light as they used to be; they were slow and measured, one step at a time.

I pulled out a magazine from the shelf, then passed through the kitchen into the living room.

That side of the house had changed considerably since I last saw it.

There was a moss-green couch near the entrance. The protruding armrests made it difficult to move around the room. Why would she put such a bulky piece of furniture here?

In the centre of the room was a kotatsu table, making the already cramped space even tighter. Though the kotatsu itself was the same one we used before, the cover was of a lattice pattern I hadn't seen. In front of the couch was a flat-screen TV, not the old tube model we had before.

'This cold is horrible.'

My mother appeared, rubbing her arms, and turned on the kotatsu heater.

I wanted to ask if she was feeling all right, but instead I found myself asking something else entirely.

'Where did this couch come from?'

'Oh that? Michieda-san from across the street didn't want it when they moved, so they brought it over.'

'Isn't it a bit too large for this room? It gets in the way when you come in.'

'Not if you turn your body sideways.'

Her response was clipped, leaving me with no choice but to say, 'Ohh-kay.'

There was an awkward silence as she slipped her feet under the kotatsu futon. She didn't seem inclined to make tea, but she wasn't throwing me out either.

I took a seat on the couch. It was comfortable and seemed of good quality.

'Is that what you came to get?' she asked.

I looked down at the issue of *Lucas* in my hand.

'Huh? Oh, yeah.'

She let out a mocking laugh.

'You really did love that magazine. I was impressed to see you so absorbed in reading, but it was just manga.'

'Manga are perfectly respectable books,' I retorted, thinking of Takaoka.

Lucas was a publication from our company. It was one of the reasons I had applied to Eiseisha to become an editor. I wanted to work for a publisher that produced such an incredible manga magazine.

Though it had always been a goal to edit a general interest magazine rather than manga, part of me was drawn to the possibility of meeting my favourite artists, perhaps even collaborating with them in some way. The more niche the artist, the more questions I wanted to ask as a fan, eager to share their brilliance with the world through my own hands.

But somewhere along the way, that passion seemed to shift into a different direction.

The more engrossed I became in my work, the more I found myself prioritizing staying ahead of new trends and understanding the public's appetites rather than what I personally thought was worthy of attention. There were times I covered topics simply because they were trending, even if I didn't understand their appeal. Of course, this was business—such decisions weren't entirely wrong. But . . .

I was certain that the pure excitement that I once felt when cracking open a book was no longer there.

An editor needs passion, or the article won't be any good.

Takaoka's words echoed in my mind.

Was I creating pages with the same passion that drove Takaoka?

Perhaps I was the one with questionable motives, forgetting those feelings and losing sight of what truly mattered.

'I have to go to the bathroom.'

My mother pushed herself up from the kotatsu, with both hands on the table.

Though her steps were steady, she briefly put a hand on the wall by the door.

'You alright?'

'Fine,' she answered immediately, then turned slightly towards me. 'Just because you're my only son doesn't mean you have to feel responsible.'

'*Huh?*'

'I know better than anyone what a hard worker you are. I couldn't do much for you. I probably made you feel miserable at times, but you did good after getting out of this rundown house. The last thing I want is to be a burden to you.'

A faint smile flickered across her face, and deep inside, my heart felt as though it were buckling under the weight of something heavy.

No, that's not it.

I didn't hate this house. I didn't hate you, Mum.

I know how much you put on your back to raise me, how much you encouraged and supported me. I do remember.

It was just that I just couldn't express it properly.

Before leaving the room, with her back to me, she said, 'So why don't we both do what we want. I want that, too.'

Before I could find anything to say in reply, she left. I glanced around the living room.

Next to the couch, facing the window, there were a couple of three-cube organizers placed next to each other. They were cluttered with books and odds and ends.

I realized the placement of these cubes was another reason the couch jutted out.

Curious about what was inside, I leaned in to take a look and let out an audible gasp.

The two bottom cubes on the window side were tightly packed with magazines.

They were issues of *Laughter*.

I pulled one out from the furthest end. The cover instantly brought back memories. It was the inaugural issue that I'd worked on as editor-in-chief.

I hardly talked to my mother about my job. I'd never told her that I had joined the editorial department of *Laughter* or that I had become editor-in-chief.

It was hard to imagine she had seen my name on the colophon, let alone that she was an avid reader of the magazine.

I heard the toilet flushing from the bathroom and hastily slipped the magazine back into place.

In my panic, a can that had been resting on top of the cubes tumbled to the floor.

Inside were some wrapped candies, which scattered everywhere.

They were the honey-flavoured candies I used to love as a kid. When I was feeling down, rather than try to console me, my mother would just toss one in my mouth, saying it was good for me. Perhaps she sucked on these, too, when she was feeling lost and alone.

My thoughts wandering, I began picking up the candies, just as my mother came back into the room. Seeing me gathering the candies in front of the organizing cubes, she must have realized I had discovered the magazines.

Mum, I'm the editor-in-chief of this magazine.

Did you know that?

Have you been reading the magazine from this far back and saving them?

How I wished I could ask her casually.

I wished she could off-handedly mention that she was.

It wouldn't be so hard, would it?

Yet, we both knew that it was precisely because it was so simple that it was impossible.

'Oh, did you have an accident? You're a clumsy one.'

Saying this, my mother moved closer to the window and pulled back the curtains to look outside.

'Another year's coming to an end.'

'Yeah.' I gave a short reply, swallowing the words that I wanted to say.

Mum, let's at least spend New Year's together.

~

When I got home, I talked to Miyako about my mother over dinner.

She mumbled quietly, 'I'm worried.'

'She seems to be struggling to keep working,' I said. 'It looks like closing the shop is unavoidable.'

'I don't know about that.'

'What?'

'It's not about the work,' Miyako said, setting down her chopsticks. 'Sunrise Cleaning is where your mother belongs. I'm not sure it's okay to suddenly take that away from her.'

'Still, it's cruel to let her keep going when her body is exhausted. No matter how much we try to help, she won't let us.'

Miyako took our bowls to the sink and stopped next to Ciao, who was grooming herself.

'Do you know what I've realized since we started living with Ciao?' Miyako said, giving the cat a rub.

'It isn't just about giving love, but accepting it, too. The kind where you trust someone and let them take care of you. The older you get, the harder that becomes.' Miyako looked up. 'Hey, why don't we go see her?'

'Now?'

It was after 8 p.m. She probably wasn't in bed yet, but it was all too sudden.

'Mum said we should do want we want, right? Well, then, that's exactly what I'm going to do.' She shot me a pointed look. 'I'd like to see Mum, right now.'

Her eyes were clear and sparkling, unclouded by doubt. My heart stirred, as if suddenly awakened.

'Okay.' I took a gulp of tea and answered, 'I'll do what I want, too.'

≈

When Miyako and I arrived at Sunrise Cleaning, we went straight to the back entrance. The light on the second floor was still on.

I could have let us in with my key, but opted to ring the doorbell instead.

It took several moments for my mother to come downstairs, and in a brusque voice, she called out, 'Who is it?' from the other side of the door. She must have been able to see us through the peephole but pretended not to know.

'It's me.'

The door clicked open, and my mother appeared, scowling.

'What is it? Did you forget something?'

'Well . . . something like that.'

She gave the two of us a look, then stepped aside to let us in.

We followed my mother into the living room and she slipped her legs under the kotatsu table.

The news was on the television.

'Let me catch the weather forecast first. It affects customer turnout.'

Miyako and I, opting not to sit at the kotatsu, sat side by side on the couch.

The weather segment before the nine o'clock news came on and proceeded at a leisurely pace. Tomorrow's forecast was cloudy with occasional clear skies. Morning and night-time temperatures would be chilly, so people should bundle up accordingly.

The meteorologist ended the forecast with a polite bow, and I got straight to the point. If I didn't come out with it directly, I wouldn't be able to take that first step.

'Listen, about closing the shop.'

My mother kept her eyes fixed on the TV, silent.

'Are you sure you want to do that?'

'That's none of your concern,' she muttered.

'But you're obviously thinking about the shop, about customer turnout.'

'Well, the store is still open tomorrow.'

'If you'd like, Miyako and I can—'

'Forget it! I don't want to run the store anymore!' she snapped, snatching the remote and turning off the TV.

Her voice trembled. 'Don't you understand? I don't want my customers to see me so old . . . so weak.'

Mum . . .

She seemed so fragile, so incredibly small.

I almost jumped up and ran to her side, but I couldn't. I was just as afraid of being pushed away as she was.

'That isn't your weakness, Mum,' Miyako said.

His mum's brows twitched slightly as I turned to Miyako.

Her voice was soft but firm. 'Your weakness isn't your age or how tired your body is. It's that you try to put on a brave face when you're hurting or lonely.'

The directness of her words caught me off guard.

Though her expression softened a little, my mother pursed her lips. 'You shouldn't go barging into people's hearts like that.'

'But I will. We've known each other for a very long time, Mum.'

A very long time?

For a moment, I was taken aback.

My mother lowered her gaze to the corner of the kotatsu table and exhaled deeply. 'Well, you're right about that.'

She smiled as if surrendering something.

Right?

What was going on?

'Ever since you two got married, you've been coming to the shop once a month with your shirts and blankets.'

Since we got married? For over twenty years?

I didn't know.

232

Miyako had been coming here by train all that time, bringing laundry, so she could check on my mother and keep our connection alive?

Then it hit me.

The collection of *Laughter* magazines, starting from the inaugural issue. It was Miyako who had told her.

'I can't just give the cold shoulder to a customer,' my mother said with a grimace, pressing her hand against her forehead.

For the past twenty years, I'd been wearing crisp shirts and sleeping in fluffy blankets that had been laundered at Sunrise Cleaning.

'That's right, I'm one of your many regular customers.' Miyako smiled.

My mother's gaze drifted, her expression softening, like the time she had been looking at the stray cat. She seemed to be remembering the customers that had come to the shop over the years.

'When you work in the same place for so long, something more than money exchanges hands,' she said. 'It's the joy of meeting people and talking to them. At some point, it becomes about more than just money. As the number of familiar faces grows, and they tell you how grateful they are that the shop is always open, or how reassuring it is to know I'm here, that's what's kept me going all these years. I felt like I had to keep going, like I had to challenge myself to see how long I could keep at it.'

My mother shrugged.

'But that's also why I thought it might be better to quit now while my body still works. So people remember the energetic, healthy version of me. You're right, I guess I have been trying to put on a brave face.'

With that, she looked down.

'But I think it's time. It's hard to think of work as something I dread.'

Miyako cast a glance at my mother's coat hanging on the wall. The grey one with the leaf embroidery.

'You know, Mum, challenges are great, but making adjustments are pretty amazing, too.'

'What?'

'It's about not staying the same but about making small improvements. Let's start by giving you a day off. It's important whether you're in your eighties or your twenties. You have to rest properly to work properly.'

My mother pouted like a child, but there was also a hint of relief in her expression.

'And you could use a hand, so I'd like to help. Whether it's at the shop or at home.'

Miyako raised her arm as if offering it.

My mother looked up at me, gauging my reaction.

I nodded emphatically.

Please, Mum. Accept our help!

Because that's the love I need from you now.

My mother's face melted into a smile.

'Well, I wonder if your hand will be as helpful as a cat's,' she said, her tongue as sharp as ever, though the corners of her eyes were glistening.

Miyako smiled, 'I'll do my best.' Then she added, 'I'm not worried. I'm sure you'll be eager to mind the store again in no time.'

~

A few days later, I called out to Takaoka, who was working at his computer.

He stopped what he was doing and came over to my desk.

I held up the proposal he'd submitted for the Ryo Sunagawa feature and said, 'This was well done. Let's refine it a bit and move forward, shall we?'

Takaoka's face instantly brightened, excitement colouring his cheeks.

'Sure thing! Thank you very much!'

It was an impressive proposal. He hadn't written it just because the artist was popular or was trending. His deep love for the manga artist and desire to share his work with a wider audience clearly came through.

I took a book out of my drawer.

'I just got this from the comics editorial department. Sample copy of the latest *Bura-man* hot off the press.'

'Whoa, no way! I've got mine pre-ordered, of course.'

Takaoka took the manga from me and happily assessed the cover before pushing it further away.

He was squinting at the fine print on the book band, his gesture oddly similar to my own.

Sensing my surprise, Takaoka said casually, 'I'm far-sighted, too. I usually wear bifocal contacts, but I got pink eye, so I'm doing without today.'

'Far-sighted? Aren't you still a bit young for that?'

'Even some elementary school kids have it these days. It's smartphone-induced far-sightedness—more and more of it in the digital age.'

'Huh,' I grunted, remembering Takaoka's quip about my needing reading glasses the other day. I guess he hadn't been mocking me. In fact, he'd probably said it out of a sense of camaraderie.

Warming to him, I continued, 'I tried bifocal contacts before, but they just seemed to make everything blurry, near and far.'

'Were they distance bifocals or near-vision bifocals?'

'Gee, I don't remember.'

It was over six years ago, so I couldn't be certain those distinctions even existed back then.

'I'm using near-vision bifocal lenses now, which are better for reading text up-close.'

'You don't say . . .'

Noticing my hesitation, Takaoka launched into an explanation.

'Contact lenses have come a long way these past few years. Now, there are lenses with different zones for various distances, and others with multifocal designs layered like rings of a tree. A while back, there weren't nearly as many options or information. I bet most people gave up before they found the right fit.'

I see . . . so there are more lenses now tailored to individual needs.

Maybe I should give them another try. The thought lifted my spirits.

Takaoka grew even more talkative.

'But what we choose to see is really more about the brain than the eyes.'

'The brain?'

'Imagine there's a bucket over on the balcony beyond a window screen. If you focus on the bucket, the screen disappears from your view. But if you look at the screen, its intricate mesh pattern comes into focus, and the bucket vanishes out of sight, and essentially out of mind. When it comes down to it, we only see what we want to see.'

'Humans are selfish that way, aren't they?' I laughed, thinking about my own habits.

Takaoka nodded. 'But that's okay. It means we're always choosing what's important and necessary in the moment. It's arrogant to expect to see each and every thing clearly.'

He was right.

As sad as it was, far-sightedness couldn't be reversed. Ageing was inevitable.

But maybe there was room for adjustment . . .

With the right tools, and the support of trusted companions.

Adapting to change was another form of recovery.

~

On a sunny Saturday, Miyako and I were on our way to Sunrise Cleaning.

After an early lunch, we planned to spend the afternoon helping my mother. I'd come along to move some furniture. The couch in the living room, for instance, was of good design and quality—comfortable enough for my mother to lie down on. The only problem was its placement.

Come to think of it, the fluorescent light in the kitchen was going out. No doubt replacing it would be difficult for her, so I planned to check the light bulb while I was there.

239

This was our approach for now.

Taking things slowly and finding ways to communicate flexibly. There was no need to rush into living together. Getting closer while maintaining some distance felt like a good way to adjust.

Miyako, walking beside me, said, 'That was delicious. I haven't had okonomiyaki in a while.'

We'd gone to a restaurant in the neighbourhood called Okonomiyaki Nikko, which we'd heard good things about. The staff there were cheerful and pleasant. A high school girl with curly hair enthusiastically attending customers had left an especially positive impression on both of us. The boy to whom she'd called out, 'Could we get some water here, please?' seemed to be about the same age.

There was still time before we were expected at the store.

'Let's make a quick detour,' I suggested to Miyako.

I finally felt ready to take her to the place that still held the sting of childhood memories, a pain I'd never been able to tell anyone.

As we approached the stone slab at the entrance, a woman with a colourful scarf wrapped around her neck emerged from the park.

'Oh, hi, Mizobata-san,' she greeted Miyako.

Miyako bowed politely, 'Are you without Mizuho-chan today?'

'Yes, I'm on my way to work.'

She smiled as she left the park.

'Is she a friend of yours?'

'That's Himura-san from the second floor. She works part-time at a boutique.'

Even though we lived in the same building, there were still so many people I'd yet to strike up a conversation with.

Yet the thought of strangers living under the same roof, each with their own hopes and burdens, warmed my heart a little.

I've got a friend in Advance Hill, too, I thought, picturing Yuya-kun with a small hint of pride.

I guided Miyako to the area beside the swings and introduced her to Kabahiko.

'He's been my buddy since I was a kid.'

'Really?'

Miyako's expression softened as she bent over to meet Kabahiko's gaze.

It was strange. I'd always thought Kabahiko wore a strained smile, like he was enduring pain, but now, for some reason, he seemed to be smiling bashfully, genuinely happy.

Maybe people really do only see what they want to see, I thought, crouching down.

Your paint-peeled body scarred with dents and scratches.

No matter how strong the winds or how heavy the rain, you stand here, steadfast.

So many hands have touched you over the years, while seeing their own reflections in you.

You must have witnessed the emotions of so many people with those eyes of yours.

There was something undeniably endearing about his weathered charm.

I found myself profoundly moved by the long, long journey that had shaped him into the handsome hippo he was today.

As we started walking out of the park, Miyako tugged at her braid, bringing its end up to her nose.

'Oh, my hair smells like okonomiyaki. Mum might not like that.'

'Really?'

I leaned in to have a sniff, but she quickly pulled away.

'Don't look at me so closely in broad daylight,'

she said, raising a hand to shield her face. 'I have all these spots and wrinkles now.'

Without thinking, I reached out and took her hand in mine. Miyako's eyes widened in surprise.

I was touching her, and she was touching me.

My steadfast companion as we grew older. Always and forever.

'I don't see it,' I said with conviction.

Really, I didn't.

My eyes weren't focused on such things.

The truth was, the closer I got to this world, the softer and more beautiful it became.

★ ★ ★ ★ ★

Michiko Aoyama was born in 1970 in Aichi Prefecture, Japan. Her English-language debut, *What You Are Looking For Is in the Library*, was shortlisted for the Japan Booksellers' Award, and was a *Time* Book of the Year, a *Times* bestseller and a *New York Times* Book of the Month. It has sold over two and a half million copies worldwide. Aoyama's latest fiction title to be translated into English and published internationally is *The Healing Hippo of Hinode Park*. Aoyama lives in Yokohama, Japan.